Packet Trade

Book One of Devi Jones' Locker

Darusha Wehm

Packet Trade
Book One of Devi Jones' Locker
by Darusha Wehm

Published by *in potentia* press

© Darusha Wehm 2016

cover illustration © NatuskaDPI

ISBN 978-0-9941332-1-2

Devi Jones' Locker:

Packet Trade
Sea Change (coming soon)

Science Fiction by M. Darusha Wehm

Beautiful Red
Children of Arkadia

Andersson Dexter novels:

Self Made
Act of Will
The Beauty of Our Weapons

Chapter One

Pirates vs. Ninjas

"One final question, Ms. Jones, and I want you to give us your gut reaction. Don't think about it, just say the first thing that comes to mind."

So far the internship interview had been tough, but more or less what I'd expected. I'd done the research. I watched the YouTube videos. I knew about Google's unanswerable questions and the lose-lose scenarios. I thought I was prepared.

The board of three interviewers were professional and they obviously knew the technical minutia of running a database cluster. It reminded me more of a final exam designed to fail half the class than anything else. That was fine. I knew my way around a database better than anywhere else, and I could talk tech until I ran out of breath. And it wasn't terribly strange that none of us knew who the company was that was running the interviews. This could be a secretive industry.

The Computer Science department vouched for them, and Anwar, my semantic web TA, had a total gleam in his eye when I told him I'd been chosen to interview. He'd had this internship himself a few years back and all he'd say about it was that it was "the best thing ever." It was the most desirable interview of them all; maybe the secrecy was part of the allure. Even so, I should have known something was up after that final question.

The interviewer, a forty-something Native American woman in a power suit, leaned in toward me and I forgot to breathe.

"Pirates or ninjas?"

What? I still don't know why I said what I did. I wonder what would have happened if I'd gone the other way. Would I be sitting in some hotel lounge in Tokyo instead of a beach bar in Nicaragua?

⚓

I wasn't looking for adventure; I certainly wasn't trying to change my life. Sometimes when things happen it all feels random and it's only later that you say, "That was it — that was the thing that made all the difference." But then sometimes it's obvious from the start that you've entered an entirely different world.

This was one of the obvious times. Condensation pooled on the plastic tablecloth at the base of the unfamiliar beer bottle. I watched as a droplet formed out of nowhere, growing until gravity took it and it rolled down the Toña label to become part of the puddle. There was a drop of sweat following the same pattern down my back. I didn't want to think about where it was ending up.

It felt like I'd been sweaty forever. It didn't seem to matter how many lukewarm showers I took, I never felt clean. I knew it was mostly humidity but it was gross. I hadn't been this hot since we'd gone to India to visit my grandparents' old village, but I'd only been seven. No soggy bra making me feel like I was wearing a wet rag around my chest.

I picked up my beer, enjoying the cool of the bottle in my hand. I don't even like beer, but *cerveza* is one of the four Spanish words I know, and doing the exchange between *córdobas* and dollars in my head told me the beer was cheap. I'd been here a couple of days — they told me to make some room in my itinerary for missed connections, so I had.

I was only in Managua long enough to find my way from the airport to the bus station, where I'd boarded what must be the fanciest bus ever made. There were attendants wearing what looked like 1970s stewardess uniforms. If I hadn't been so groggy, I might have wondered if I was hallucinating. The reckless driving of the conductor was real enough, though. I nodded off for a while in the plush seats, then after what seemed like no time I was disgorged in the bustling metropolis of San Juan del Sur.

I don't know what I expected, but the few tidy blocks of bars, restaurants, hostels and surf gear stores that made up the town wasn't it. A loud laugh from the next table startled me, and I looked over at a group of surfers — probably Americans. I looked down at the skinny legs sticking out of my khaki shorts, the battered paperback soaking up the condensation on the tablecloth, the hand-me-down duffel bag at my feet.

What the hell was I doing here? I slugged on the beer and tried to ignore its lemonade-gone-bad taste.

⚓

A shadow fell over me and I looked up. It was much brighter outside than it was in the bar and I couldn't make out the person blocking the light.

"Are you Jones? Uh, Duh-vie Jones?" It wasn't the worst attempt at my first name I'd ever heard, and at least he tried.

"That's me," I said, "and it's Devi. Like the boy's name."

"Davy?" he echoed and I thought I caught a smile forming on his face.

"Yeah. Are you the captain?"

"No." The smile fully blossomed. He moved out of the sun and I got a look at him. Late twenties, maybe. Blond hair, deep tan, but he somehow didn't look anything like the surfer dudes that filled the beaches and hostels here. "I'm the mate, Isaac. Skipper's talking to the *Capitanía* getting your paperwork settled." Was I supposed to know what that meant? Was I supposed to have done something? He didn't say anything else about it, instead he looked down at my bag. "That's all your stuff?"

I nodded. My heart started to bang, the sound of blood rushed in my head and I realized that this was it. I was really doing this. I was going to get on a boat with a stupid name and a bunch of strangers and sail away. I don't know if panic showed in my face, but Isaac didn't look fazed.

"Glad to see someone who actually follows the instructions. You wouldn't believe the stuff some of the people we've had come through have tried to bring aboard. The *Bucket* ain't a cruise ship." He looked at the battered watch on his wrist. "We'll be heading out next morning, but it's good to have a night aboard before we get under way. You checked out of your hostel already?"

"Yeah," I said, fighting the urge to run.

"Well," he said, "we can get going any time you want. Though, if it's okay with you, I've got a mad hankering for a cheeseburger and this place does a good one. You mind if I get a bite before we go?"

"Um, sure?"

"Great! Want anything?" My stomach wasn't happy at all with the half a beer I'd drunk, and the thought of a burger did nothing to help, but I was really thirsty and there was no way I was finishing that beer.

"You think they have some kind of juice?"

He laughed and said, "Oh, yeah. They have *all* the juice. Any preference?"

"Anything but apple."

"Gotcha." He ambled off and I watched him talk to the woman behind the bar in easy Spanish.

This whole thing wasn't like me at all. I wasn't ever one of those kids who was scared of the roller coaster or jumping off the high diving board, but the thought of taking a year off to go backpacking around Europe never appealed. If someone had told me ten months ago that I'd be sitting in a bar in Nicaragua with a man I'd never met before, watching him devour a burger before getting on a sailboat where I was going to spend the next nine months... well. I probably would have rolled my eyes and walked away. And yet, here I was, watching Isaac eat while I drank the best tasting glass of juice I'd ever had.

"You've got an auspicious name," he said, taking a breather from eating. "Sailors are a superstitious lot, but I think it bodes well."

"My name?"

"Sure. Davy Jones — you know, like *Pirates of the Caribbean*?"

"Yeah, I've heard of it," I said. You don't get to be nearly twenty and have a name like mine without hearing it all. Usually it's that guy from The Monkees, though. "Isn't it kind of a bad thing, though?"

He shrugged. "Well, I've got not desire to be visiting Davy Jones' Locker, but there's more to it than that. Supposedly it's named after this guy who was an incredible seaman—" He grinned, waiting for me to giggle, which I kind of wanted to do, but stopped myself. "You spend much time on the water before?"

I shook my head. "They told me experience wasn't necessary. For the sailing part."

"Yeah, that's what my people are for. You won't be able to avoid learning a thing or two about boats, though. And with a name like yours, you should be nautical." He wiped his fingers on a thin paper napkin, then balled it up and tossed it on to his spotless plate.

I had a moment of panic. Had I been offered this position just because of my name? Was it possible that the selection committee was as superstitious as Isaac seemed to be? I'd been sure it was because I aced the database tuning test — I'd been totally in the zone when I was working on it and I'd gotten it purring like a kitten. Anwar had been so impressed when I told him I'd been called back.

"It's a real coup," he'd said. "Half the guys in the program would kill for this spot. Don't fuck it up."

I don't think I really believed it was for real, even when Anwar finally told me a bit about his placement. Who would put a commercial server on a sailboat? And then hire a student intern as an onsite administrator? It's nonsense. But how could I say no?

"So, you ready to see the *Bucket*?" Isaac asked. I didn't want to tell him the truth, that I was most certainly not ready, I'd never be ready, I'd made a terrible mistake. I'd thought I could handle it, that it would be make for a great story. But now that I was here, and the full force of how utterly and completely weird this was came over me... nope. Not ready at all.

But, what could I do? I wasn't about to let everyone down — my parents, my teachers — just because I was freaked out. If I was expected to get on the boat, I'd get on the boat. That was me: always meeting or exceeding expectations. So, I forced a smile and nodded.

Isaac must have seen something in my face, because he picked up my duffel and threw his arm around my shoulder. "She's a sturdy ship and she takes care of all aboard. You're gonna be fine, kid." Then he let me go and walked out the door into the heat and humidity of the afternoon.

⚓

Byte Bucket was anchored way out in the bay, past dozens of rusty fishing boats. The surf was down that day according to the talk in the hostel, but the boats were all still lifting and falling in the swell, so I couldn't even make out what Isaac was pointing at for a while. It took me ages to pick it out, because it looked like a generic modern sailboat. I'd been expecting something out of *Master and Commander*, all square sails and hemp rope and guys swinging across the poop deck.

"There she is." The pride in his voice was strangely reassuring. "Home sweet home. The tender's tied up over by the old cannery." I must have had a blank expression, because he explained, "The dinghy. How we get out to the boat and back again."

"Oh." He pointed down a dusty road toward a squat concrete building. The demarcation between the tourist centre of town and the commercial harbour was obvious. The buildings became more utilitarian, the paved road abruptly ended. After a few paces we came across a chain link fence bordering a small boatyard, with several fishing boats shored up with bits of wood and concrete blocks. There was a lone sailboat, its mast on the ground beside it.

"Ahoy, Pedro!"

A head popped out of a hole in the sailboat and the wrinkly face broke into a smile.

"Zak! I saw *Byte Bucket* at anchor and I wondered if

I'd see you today. This the latest greenie?"

Isaac nodded and I raised a hand. "Hi. I'm Devi."

"Good to know you, Devi. Where you all headed?"

"Uh..." I had no idea.

"We're off to Santa Elena in the morning," Isaac said. He gave the dismembered boat an exaggerated once over. "You're leaving any day now, too, I see."

"Don't be a smart-ass," Pedro said, good-naturedly. "*Dream Rider*'ll be as good as new when I'm done here. I'm just waiting on a part I'm having shipped down from the States. Next time I see you it'll be in the South Pacific somewhere."

Isaac laughed and said, "You bet, Pedro. Lookin' good." He started off walking down the dusty street, but I found myself frozen in place. Holy shit. The South Pacific.

The boat's planned itinerary had been part of the orientation package I'd received, scant and weird though it had been. There was a copy of the database architecture scheme, which was the only thing that made any sense to me. The rest of the package was a paperback copy of the Neal Stephenson book *Cryptonomicon*, a DVD of some old movie called *Captain Ron* and a USB stick with the complete discography of Jimmy Buffett. And the itinerary, of course.

Growing up in a suburb of Vancouver, I'd always assumed I was familiar with lots of faraway places. Walking down any street you could see people from all over the world. But at home in Burnaby, the list of locations on the itinerary had been so exotic they were practically meaningless. I'd never even heard of half of these places. Playas del Coco. Isla Isabela. Mo'orea. Suwarrow. They might as well have given me a list of alien planets we'd be visiting in our pan-galactic star cruiser.

"What an opportunity to see the world," my mom said, reading over my shoulder like she always did, driving me crazy. "You'll be going places most people only dream of."

My dad had been more practical. "This will look great on your CV. Where did they say previous students ended up working?"

"Amazon, Tesla," I'd answered though I knew he remembered. Mom and Dad had been thrilled when I'd been accepted by the program. I guess they assumed that anything endorsed by the university must be legitimate. I suppose I thought so too, or I wouldn't have even applied. But now, standing on a dirt road with a frankly deranged-looking Pedro grinning at me, watching the only person I knew here walk toward a decrepit concrete wharf where some dodgy-looking open boats were tied, I was pretty certain that I was going to die.

"Better get going." I jumped at the sound of Pedro's voice. "You miss your ride and you'll have to swim." He grinned and I noticed that most of his teeth were not there.

I mumbled something and scurried to catch up to Isaac, who still had my bag of stuff. I strongly suspect that if I'd been carrying my own bag, I'd have turned and run in the other direction.

⚓

Byte Bucket's dinghy didn't look anything like most of the boats tied up at the wharf: open, canoe-shaped boats of rough fibreglass, mostly with large outboard bolted to the back. Then locals called them *pangas* and they were everywhere. The dinghy was completely different — it wasn't new, but it was a modern-looking inflatable thing that looked familiar. I watched Isaac spring into it with barely a hint of motion, carefully placing my duffel on a seat so it wouldn't get wet. I stepped onto the side of the boat and felt it give significantly under my foot. I jerked my leg back on to the dock and saw the boat that had once looked so large appear to shrink before my eyes as it wobbled side to side.

"Come on," Isaac said, "get in. It's not going to capsize, promise."

I gingerly put my foot on the side, still nervous at how much the boat moved when I touched it. I knelt on the concrete beside the boat, and slowly inched my way into it. I knew I looked ridiculous, but I was still shaking once I got completely on board and seated in the middle. Isaac looked at me and smiled, and I got the feeling this wasn't an unusual experience for him, shepherding the new kid.

"You'll get the hang of it," he said. "Once you've fallen overboard a few times it stops being such a big deal. Unless you've got your laptop with you. Then it pretty much sucks." He didn't wait for me to answer, but instead arched back and yanked on a cord. The engine fired to life and the next thing I knew we were flying over the water and away from shore.

It was terrifying and exhilarating. I turned to look behind us and in the churning water of our wake I saw my last chance to get out of this dissolve into spray.

It turned out that *Byte Bucket* wasn't a generic modern sailboat after all. I couldn't make it out from a distance, but as we approached the anchored boat I began to notice that there was some kind of design on the side. It was difficult to see with the movement of the boat I was on and the rising and falling of the sea, but when I finally saw the image resolve I half gasped/half laughed.

"Is that—?"

Isaac turned back to me, his grin echoing the image on the side of the boat. "A shark painted on the hull? Hell, yeah, it's a shark. Got it done in New Zealand a couple of seasons ago." He turned to look at the boat, then back at me. "Isn't it awesome?!"

I couldn't deny it — it was awesome, if a bit tacky. Though with a name like *Byte Bucket*, I guess they weren't too concerned with class. Even I could tell this wasn't the yacht club set. As we got up close I realized that my estimate of the size of the boat was off, too. It was like passing a wall as we drove along the side of the boat to pull up to a platform set into the back near the water. Isaac tied the boats together one handed, then turned to me.

"You get off first," he said. "Try to time the swells and remember: 'one hand for you; one hand for the ship'." I'd thought getting on the boat at the wharf was hard, but that was nothing compared to this. The boat we were on was lurching in the swell and the big boat wasn't still either. The squeak of the two boats rubbing against each other didn't help. Isaac just waited patiently as I grabbed at various nautical things I didn't recognize to try and make myself steady. Finally I managed to lever myself out of the boat and on to the platform.

"Good job," Isaac said, hoisting my duffel on to his shoulder and seemingly effortlessly shifting it and himself from boat to boat. "This isn't an ideal spot for your first dinghy transfer, but the good news is it'll get easier from here on in." He clapped me on the shoulder and gestured up a short ladder. "Go aboard; I'll be there in a sec."

I climbed up the ladder to find myself at the back of the boat. Compared to what I'd imagined, it was immense. I followed the line of some metal wire near me up to the mast, which seemed to be impossibly tall. I began to get a little dizzy.

"She's something else, eh?" Isaac said, handing me my bag. I winced as I stubbed my toe on some mysterious object; everywhere I stepped I banged into something. There were ropes coiled all over the floor, and metal poles holding up every manner of things I didn't recognize. Except the solar panels — I recognized those and they were everywhere. There was some kind of hut built behind the mast and its entire roof was covered in photovoltaic cells. Plus an entire array of them was perched on each side.

"You must generate a lot of power," I said.

"Yeah," Isaac answered, "but it's never enough. We'd

be a power hungry boat even without your lot, but those machines eat a ton."

"According to the specs, the servers you're running are among the efficient I've ever seen."

"That may be, but they still draw more amp hours than the rest of the boat combined, not counting the freezer."

"I never really thought about it," I said as I carefully picked my way around ropes and wires, "but we're totally off-grid out here."

Isaac laughed so hard he had to stop walking. "Devi, most of the time we're going to be farther away from land than the gang on the International Space Station. A ship at sea is the most remote place a person can be, aside from Everest. And I'm not that sure about Everest." He must have seen the look on my face, because he took a step toward me. "Don't panic. Remoteness is good, sometimes. And you aren't alone — there are a half dozen other people out here with you. Don't get me wrong; it's going to be a big learning curve, but you'll be fine. Now let's get down below and meet the crew."

⚓

Once we ducked in through the door to the hut, everything started to feel a bit more normal. The room was more like a small dance hall than anything else: hardwood floors, a wide bar, even a large flat screen TV on the back wall. There were built-in couches along the sides and a man and woman about my age were sitting on one. They looked up as we entered.

"Hey guys, this is Devi, the new co-op student," Isaac said. "This is Martin and Tulia."

"Hi." I lifted a hand in greeting and tried to be cool.

The guy was around my age, his pale face currently a shade of pink that I didn't think was sunburn. Tulia was about Martin's height and age, but appeared much more in control of herself. Maybe it was her size that gave her an air of formidability. I'd gone to junior high with a Hawaiian girl who looked similar and I wondered where she was from. The company who hired me — and, presumably, everyone else on board — was run by a couple of Americans but had offices in Sweden and the US. They could employ people from anywhere.

Isaac continued the introduction. "These two are our regular crew, but Tulia is a whiz electrician. If you've got power issues, go see her."

"*When* you've got power issues," she said, rolling her eyes at Isaac. "Nice to meetcha. I've been talking Martin out of desertion. Again."

"I'm not deserting," he said, a twinge of whine in his voice.

"I know," Tulia said, all smug satisfaction. She stood, ignoring Martin's scowl. "Let me show you around. Most things are pretty unisex around here, but there are a few girl things I should tell you about."

I looked back at Isaac, who nodded. "I'll catch up with you in a bit," he said, handing me my duffel. "I better have a chat with Martin, here."

"I'm not deserting," I heard him protest as Tulia led

me down the tight corridor. She laughed.

"He's only been aboard a few months and we haven't even put out to sea yet, not really. He's freaking out over nothing."

"He could leave, though, couldn't he?" I was having visions of press-gangs and keel-haulings, even though I wasn't exactly sure what either of those terms meant.

"Sure," Tulia said, as we emerged into a large room flanked by three-high bunks. "He's got a contract, but we're not indentured or anything. He likes the attention, I think." She waggled her eyebrows at me then flung open a door to what I thought was a closet. Her round body nearly filled the doorway.

"This is the head," she said.

"The what?"

"The toilet," she explained, a smile creeping around the corners of her mouth. "You ever use a marine toilet before?" I shook my head, mortified that I was about to be educated on how to go to the bathroom. She backed up, gesturing for me get into the small room. She pointed at things from outside the door.

"It's no big deal, just turn this switch for water and pump this handle to flush. The switch goes over here if you want to pump out the water to make it dry." Her expression grew serious. "And you do want to do that. The last thing anyone wants is seawater — or *whatever* — all over the head. But the most important thing is that nothing goes down here unless you ate it first or it's toilet paper. And not much of that, either."

"Okay," I said, wishing I were anywhere else. I could see why Martin wanted to desert.

"Seriously, DO NOT flush a tampon down here. You clog it, you fix it, okay?"

Oh, god. I nodded.

"It's not so bad, really. You'll get used to it, I promise." She hustled me out the tiny, complicated bathroom and we turned down another narrow corridor. "Showers are down here. There are four of them, and we have a schedule. There usually isn't hot water, but it doesn't matter because the tank water is as warm as the ocean. And you can't just run the water like you do ashore. You get in, get wet, turn off the water, soap and shampoo and whatever, then rinse off. That's it."

"Like camping," I said, feeling like an idiot.

Tulia didn't laugh, though. "Yeah, exactly. The boat's kind of like a big tent. Actually, if you think of it that way it seems really luxurious — running water, a flush toilet, a soft bed."

"Speaking of which..."

"I don't know which bunk is yours, but crew all sleep in that room we passed."

"All of us?"

"The captain and the mate each have their own staterooms and the cook sleeps by the galley."

"I mean..." I swallowed, thinking about what it would be like. I shared an apartment with my brother Nico, but that was different. I'd never slept in the same room as a guy before. Except camping with my family when we were kids, but that didn't count. "That works okay?"

"Sure. Like I said, we're pretty unisex around here. There just isn't enough room for two crew quarters, and since we're all on weird shifts anyway it doesn't matter. It only gets crowded in there when we're in port, and some of us stay ashore if we get lucky." Her eyebrows went again and I couldn't help but smile.

She was cute in a coarse kind of way, but I stamped on that feeling, hard. I couldn't imagine the appalling drama of a shipboard romance, and I wasn't prepared to get involved with anyone anyway. Not after Jeannette.

I forced myself to stop thinking about it and racked my brain for other questions I should ask. After the toilet lesson it became obvious that I didn't even know what I didn't know.

"Uh, what about food?"

"Galley's though there," she pointed and I couldn't tell if it was yet another hallway or one we'd already come through. "I wouldn't worry about it for now, there's four squares a day if you want them, so you shouldn't go hungry."

"Four?"

"Yeah, there's a fourth meal for those of us on night watch. This is the first boat I've worked on that does it, but it's pretty awesome."

"Night watch? We have to stay up all night?"

"Wow, you are new." Tulia started walking and I fell into step behind her. "When we're under way there's always someone on deck, always someone around to do whatever. The captain and mate take turns and one of us is always around. That means all night, too. So, night watch."

"You can't just anchor for the night?"

Tulia laughed again. "Nowhere to anchor in the middle of the ocean, kid. When we're on a passage we'll be at sea for days. Weeks sometimes. This is it." She banged the flat of her hand along the wall of the boat. "This is home."

⚓

Tulia brought me back to the large room — the "main salon," apparently — and just as I'd sat down Isaac appeared from some hidden doorway. I despaired of ever finding my way around the place.

"Skipper's coming aboard soon, so I'm going to show you your bunk before chow time. You can meet everyone else then, okay?"

I nodded and stood. I hadn't noticed the movement of the boat before, and I didn't exactly notice it then, either. I just fell over. I flopped back on to the couch, stunned.

Isaac chuckled. "You'll get your sea legs soon, don't worry. Just remember: one hand for yourself, one hand for the ship." He pointed to a neatly recessed handrail above the couch. I looked around and saw that they were dotted all over the walls at about eye level. I grabbed it and levered myself up, and found that the floor was, indeed, slowly rocking. It was unnerving, yet strangely comfortable.

I managed to grab my bag from the floor and sling it over my shoulder, then hang on to a nearby handrail before falling over again. I followed Isaac, who ignored his own advice about holding on to something and walked easily, while I hand-over-handed it along the corridor. I felt dumb, but stayed on my feet.

We got to the bunk room and he pointed to a curtained-off area near the corner. "If you want to move later that's fine, we've got spares. But a lower bunk is best to start." I agreed, and pulled back the curtains. There was a mattress that was smaller than a single bed but bigger than a cot, with a net near the foot and a small cupboard built into the wall. I stuffed my bag into the net, then turned back to Isaac.

He showed me how to secure the curtain at the bottom and sides so it would stay closed. "For privacy?" I asked.

"That, too. Mostly it's to keep you from falling out in a seaway."

"I never really thought about the moving around aspect of being on a boat," I said. "I always pictured it as kind of a motel."

"Like I said, the *Bucket* ain't a cruise ship, and even they rock and roll a little bit. It's an adjustment, but it's worth it. C'mon, let's see if everyone's back from shore leave and get some food. That burger was good, but it wasn't enough."

We left the bunk room from the door opposite the

one that led to the main salon — I was starting to make a mental map of the layout. In a few steps there was a ladder that led down into a very comfortable area with a large table and benches, all bolted to the floor. Several people were seated at the table, including Tulia and Martin, and they all stopped talking when we arrived.

"Everyone, this is Devi."

The table broke into a discordant chorus of greetings and I waved at them all weakly. "Hey," I said and pointed at a spot next to Martin. He nodded and I climbed over the bench to sit, nearly falling into his lap in the process. I was blushing and felt like an idiot, but while I saw a few smiles around the table, no one laughed at me. Tulia gave me a look that I didn't really understand, but I knew I'd done something she didn't like.

"This is a shitty anchorage," the other woman said, though she said it like it was just a fact rather than a complaint. "It's never calm out here. Wait 'til we get to Santa Elena, you'll think you're living in a concrete bunker it's so flat."

"It's not always like this?" I asked, surreptitiously hanging on to the side of the table to keep from slipping off the seat.

"Nah," she said. "This is, thankfully, unusual. I'm Christine, by the way." She stuck her hand out for me to shake.

"What do you do around here?"

"Replace the transmission oil cooler, mostly." There were a couple of chuckles. "I babysit the iron jenny."

"Uh—"

"The engine," Martin explained.

"Oh," I said, wondering if there was a hope of ever understanding a tenth of this lingo. I turned to the guy on Christine's left. He was older than everyone else by anywhere from five to thirty-five years, with long, dirty blond hair and the kind of tan you get from working outdoors. I'd pegged him as the captain when I sat down and now I wasn't sure what to say. Would I have to call him "sir?"

He put me out of my misery. "Hiya. I'm Jim Houghton but you can call me Jimmy; everybody does. I probably forgot more about boats than they know all together, so you have any questions about sailing a rhumb line versus a great circle route, I'm your man. I don't know nothing about your computer stuff, though, so you're on your own there." He stood and walked around a corner and I heard some banging and *sotto voce* cursing.

"He seems nice enough," I said.

"Jimmy?" Christine said. "Yeah, he's all right. Likes to tell us all about how much better cruising was back in the day, when you go to the islands and the locals treat you like family because they've never had tourists before, that sort of thing. But he does amazing things with canned food and makes hot meals even in a gale, so I can't complain."

That didn't make much sense to me, but I didn't get a chance to ask for clarification before Jimmy yelled, "I heard that!" then came back out with a large tray of rolls in one hand and a big pot in the other.

"Well, you are the best ship's cook I've ever seen," she retorted, grabbing a roll and tossing it back and forth between her hands. "Ooh, hot!"

"You're the *cook*?" I said, then immediately regretted it.

"Who did you think I was, the skipper?" This time everyone did laugh. "Nah, Mat'll be here soon enough. Captain doesn't like to miss meals."

As if on cue, a rustling sound came from a nearby hallway. A young woman who looked only a few years older than me burst into the room. She was wearing a tie-dyed tee-shirt and a pair of those baggy pants you see people selling at hippy farmers' markets. She reminded me of one of my dad's Rastafarian cousins.

"Captain on deck," Jimmy shouted and raised his hand in a salute.

"Stop scaring the new crew." She spoke with a slight accent I couldn't quite place but gave me a strong Caribbean vibe about her. She looked me over and I felt like a soldier on inspection. "Devi Jones, I presume?"

She pronounced my name right, I'll give her that. Of course, that just made Jimmy say, "You gotta be kidding me."

"Shut up, Jimmy," the captain said. "Good to meet you, Devi. I'm Mat Larousse. Since you'll want to know but be afraid to ask, the Mat's short for Mathilde, but don't call me that. Call me Mat when we're hanging out, and Captain or Skipper when we're working. Got it?"

"Uh huh," I stammered.

She slipped into a free spot across from me and turned to Jimmy. "So, what's for dinner?"

⚓

Dinner was good, both the food and the conversation. It seemed over in a flash, between people asking me about myself and spending the rest of the time trying to take everything in. Jimmy was clearing away the plates when Mat cleared her throat. The tenor of the room changed slightly and she said, "We're all checked out with the Port Captain, so we're aboard for the night. I'm planning to get under way some time in the morning, not too early. We'll make Santa Elena by nightfall, so this should be a nice easy run. We'll spend a few days at anchor at Elena, getting Devi used to the boat and hopefully letting her get our cargo back up and running."

Everyone nodded. I worked to parse what she'd said. "Uh, Captain?" She raised her eyebrows as if to indicate that I should go on. "What did you mean, exactly, 'back up and running'?"

"Out last IT crew member went ashore a few weeks ago and when I was in town I got a message from head office that our node is out of service, whatever that means. Nothing good, I assume." She broke open a roll and mopped up the dregs of her stew. "I'm afraid you're being thrown in at the deep end, Devi. The system is down and you're the only one aboard who has the slightest clue how to fix it."

My job on the boat was to take care of the racks that were our part of the RRD servers. It was a bizarre system — a group of servers on the *Byte Bucket*, another set on the top of a mountain in Europe, another bunch on an orbiting satellite, and a few other equally difficult locations. But that was the point: *Really Remote Desktop*. It was the most inefficient system I could imagine, but it was cool. There was a definite market. The ad campaign was slick — keep your data safe from prying eyes on our data haven cloud servers. It was all just a gimmick, of course, but at least they were clear that's what it was.

And the work would be a challenge. Keeping a regular cloud server up and running wasn't exactly easy, but it was a known quantity. Keeping one going over an unreliable network surrounded by saltwater on a moving vessel? That was bleeding edge stuff.

At least, that's what I'd told myself when I got the orientation package. The other offer I'd had was working in a glass and steel tower downtown for a giant megalopolis. As my dad said, I've got a lifetime ahead of me to work for The Man.

"You're young, now is when you should be doing crazy stuff. And this way you get to have an adventure, and they pay you!"

It was barely pay, but I got room and board and a story to tell. "You'll regret it your whole life if you don't go," Mom said. "Who gets this kind of opportunity at your age? At any age?"

The only person who even came close to suggesting I might turn it down was Jeannette. But even she admitted that her reservations were just because she didn't want me to go. So she broke up with me instead. Did I ever really have a choice? Everyone I knew wanted me to get on the *Byte Bucket* and sail away for nearly a year. It never mattered for a second what I wanted to do.

⚓

Part of me expected that we'd break out a keg of rum and sing sea shanties, but after dinner the crew broke up and everyone just did their own thing. It reminded me of when we visited my dad's family in Trinidad. Martin and Jimmy put on a DVD in the main salon, Tulia went up on deck with a beer and Christine went to her bunk with a book. I don't know what happened to the captain and Isaac — I got the impression they left us to ourselves most of the time.

I went up and tried to watch the movie, but there weren't enough explosions and car chases for my frame of mind, so I made my excuses and climbed up above decks. The night was still warm, though a strong breeze came from the direction of town. The lights of the waterfront bars were twinkling and I thought I could hear music from one of them. I turned away and my breath caught. It was like I imagine being in space must be like — the deepness of the dark. The moon wasn't up yet, or maybe it was a new moon? Either way, there was only a slight difference in the shade of black to delineate where the sea gave way to the sky. Though as my eyes adjusted I noticed that the sky was full of stars. More stars than I'd ever seen before. It was breathtaking.

"Thought you'd be watching the movie." Tulia's voice startled me.

"Couldn't get into it," I said. "Besides, who'd watch a movie when there's this?"

She didn't answer and I wondered if I'd done something to upset her. Then she said, "It's a nice night, all right."

"Yeah," I said, not turning away from the view. "Is it always like this?"

"Nah. Sometimes it's cloudy, or further north you get fog. But there's nothing like a night out at sea. If you think this is something, wait until we get a few miles offshore."

I stared out at the stars for a while. "Night watch, eh?"

"Yeah," Tulia said. "Like everything else around here there are good parts and bad parts." She sounded a little sad, but she didn't elaborate and I didn't ask.

We sat in silence staring at the stars for a while before she said goodnight and went down below.

⚓

I didn't see a clock, but it couldn't have been that late when I decided to turn in. I was bone tired, though. I'd mostly been sitting around all day but I felt like I'd done a tough hour at the gym. I took my stuff into one of the toilets — *heads*, I mentally corrected myself. The pump mechanism wasn't as complicated as I'd feared, and I changed into light PJs then padded back to my bunk. There was barely enough light to see by from the hall and I fumbled with the catch on the curtains. I finally got it open and crawled into the bunk. It had seemed tiny when Isaac showed it to me, but once I was in it wasn't so bad. I could sit up and there was a reading light and small fan near my pillow. On the side of the wall was a sliding door with a shallow cupboard behind that ran the length of the berth. I could cram a lot of stuff in there, I realized, and the net at my feet held my whole bag anyway.

I could live here, I thought to myself, at least for nine months. It was going to be okay. Maybe not great, maybe not even good, but tolerable. I lay down and shut off the light, worried that I'd never fall asleep in such a strange place. I was out before I knew it.

It didn't last, though. I woke up sometime in the night in a panic, wrapped up in the sheet and covered in sweat. I couldn't remember where the light switch was, and I couldn't figure out how to open the curtains. I must have been banging around in there for a while when the curtains somehow magically parted and a dark shape whispered, "You okay?"

"Yeah," I whispered back, though it wasn't exactly true. "Just. Hot."

"Use the fan," the voice said. "It's what it's for. And don't worry about it. I freaked out the first few nights, too. It's kinda claustrophobic in these things. I just leave the curtains loose when we aren't under way."

By now I'd recognized my liberator as Martin. I was equally grateful of the help and mortified by needing him to help me escape from my bed.

"Thanks," I said, smoothing the sheet and trying to maintain as much dignity as I could in sweaty pajamas. "Sorry if I woke you."

"Naw, I was just coming to bed. See you in the morning." I could see his shadow moving, but I still couldn't really make anything out. Hopefully he was just as night blind as me. I groped around for the fan switch and got it turned on. The fan was surprisingly quiet and made a noticeable difference. I closed but didn't latch the curtains and lay back down. This time it took forever to fall asleep.

⚓

After my middle-of-the-night excitement, I was completely zonked out when someone shook my shoulder to wake me.

"We're weighing anchor in a couple of hours." It was Christine and I got myself all caught up in my sheets again as I tried to get out of the bunk. "Hey, don't hurt yourself or anything, it's not like we need you up there." Ouch. I wondered if she meant that so sound as cold as it did.

"Well, then, why'd you wake me up?" It came out with more snark than I'd intended, but I'd never been my best in the morning.

"Sorry, your highness. I just figured you'd want to

see this. Besides, I think they want you getting that system back up sooner rather than later." She swept out of the bunk room and I regretted the entire conversation immediately. The last thing I needed was an enemy.

Ugh. I'd somehow managed to completely forget that the *Bucket*'s set of servers was offline. If only I'd had a decent sleep.

I checked the list and it wasn't my shower day, so I splashed some water on myself and threw on a short sleeved collared shirt and light pants, hoping there wasn't more of a dress code than I'd already seen. I made my way to the galley (I was starting to get the lingo down) and saw that I needn't have worried. The Captain and Isaac were there, poking at a tablet. She wore an ancient-looking tank top and cut-offs, and Isaac looked frankly bizarre in a pair of soccer shorts and an unbuttoned Hawaiian shirt.

They looked up when I came and both grinned. "This isn't an office job, Devi," Mat said. "It's hot and you're going to get saltwater on yourself. Save your good clothes for shore leave and go put on something comfortable."

"Okay," I said. "Is it safe to have breakfast before I change?"

Isaac laughed. "Sure. There's bread and jam and cereal and there may even be some fresh milk left." He jerked his head toward Jimmy's domain. "Help yourself. There's no out of bounds on the *Bucket*, not for you. We stay away from your servers, though. Don't worry about that."

"Yeah, that." I ducked into the next room and found half a loaf of bread on the counter along with an assortment of spreads. I grabbed a couple of slices with jam and came back to the table. "So, I'm the only tech on board, right?" Nods. "You know I've never worked in... this kind of facility before."

"Not many have," Mat said. "It's not as bad as it seems. Eat, and I'll show you the locker."

After I had some food in my stomach, I asked, "So, when we are sailing, do we have to take vitamins or anything."

Mat shrugged. "You can if you want. Do whatever you usually do. If there's anything in particular you need, stock up the next time we're shopping."

"No, I'm okay, but, uh, what about... scurvy?"

She was trying to not laugh at me, that was obvious. She failed, but at least she made the effort. Isaac came to my rescue.

"That's not going to be a problem. We will be in port more often than we're not and people eat everywhere. In most of the places we'll be fresh fruit is the easiest thing in the world to come by. Even when we're at sea a long time, we'll be eating fine, I promise. This is the 21st century, even if sometimes it's hard to tell out here."

I looked through the galley hatch at the large bowl of fruit on the counter and the fresh vegetables stowed neatly in a net. Right. Time to forget what I thought I knew and concentrate on what I did know. I finished breakfast and asked Mat to give me the tour.

There was a trapdoor in the floor of the main salon which led down a ladder to a room the size of a generous walk-in closet. There were a couple of racks with servers bolted to the walls — "bulkheads," Mat corrected. A series of fat power cables snaked off through a conduit and there was a robust laptop in a workstation with a built-in seat. It looked oddly comfortable.

"The workstation's gimballed," Mat said, "and the laptop can be secured with these straps." She pulled a couple of bits of webbing from a hatch and hooked them over the base of the laptop.

"Gimballed?"

She popped a couple of latches and I found myself swinging back and forth. The entire unit was on a horizontal pivot. "In a seaway it makes things a lot more comfortable." She stopped the motion and secured the workstation again. "We run a satellite connection when we're at sea and have our own cell aboard for when we're near shore. As far as I know we've got a connection, but there's something screwy here and the bits aren't getting in and out properly. Or so I'm told. This isn't my area." She grinned. "But it can wait another hour and you might as well see how the boat works. Let's go above decks and get this show on the road!"

⚓

Everyone was above decks: Isaac by the big wheel, Mat hanging out by the mast and the others in various locations on deck. I found a place to sit that was out of the way. Tulia came by with a contraption that she showed me how to put on. It was kind of like a climbing harness but less constricting. It didn't look like any life jacket I'd ever seen but she told me it was a PFD — a personal flotation device.

"It'll automatically inflate if you fall overboard," she said, "but don't test it out, okay?" I tightened the straps a bit more around my waist.

Martin was at the front of the boat making hand signals and I saw Isaac gesture back. A whirring engine noise started and I could see that we were moving slowly forward. "Are we under way?"

"Not yet," Tulia said. "They're just pulling up the anchor." This went on for about a minute, then there was more gesturing and a clang. Isaac pulled at a lever. We began to accelerate, but it was very slow and even. Mat and Christine were doing something by the mast and then a huge sail began to rise. Isaac spun the wheel, and we turned around while the boat began to lean over. A lot. I hung on to the nearest metal post and looked over at Tulia.

She must have seen the panic in my eyes. "It's okay; this is normal. The boat heels over when we're pointing close to the wind. It's supposed to happen."

"If you say so." I hung on to the post for dear life, completely mystified that the rest of them could walk around on this leaning platform like it was nothing. We kept turning and the sail went out and the more we turned the more level the world became. Eventually I found the courage to let go, but I wasn't about to try walking anywhere.

"Ready the fore'sl," Mat yelled and Tulia began to do things with ropes nearby. I watched her pull a rope around a winch for what seemed like forever, then there was a huge *thwang* sound and we noticeably sped up. She stuck a handle in the winch and turned it several times, then sat back looking slightly smug.

"That's sailing."

I looked around and saw two billowing white sails and could see that we were moving pretty quickly though the water.

"It's just the wind moving us?"

"Yup. Awesome, isn't it."

It seemed mostly terrifying to me. But terrifying is a kind of awesome, right?

⚓

Once I got used to moving around, I found Mat reading a book near the back of the boat and guessed that she wasn't busy. "Captain?"

She dog-eared her page. "What's up?"

"I know I need to get the servers back online but—" I felt the boat sway beneath me and grabbed at a nearby pole.

"It can wait until we're anchored; don't worry. Eventually you'll have to get used to working down below when we're under way, but this isn't supposed to be a trial by fire. Sorry, it's bad timing. When a new tech comes on board the idea is that we ease you into it with a couple of nice pleasure cruises and some easy maintenance. It's not your fault that the system went down. The whole point of the system having so many nodes is so that there's no one point of failure. It can wait."

"Thanks."

"Have a seat." She moved a pile of ropes and made space on a thin cushion. It wasn't exactly soft, but it wasn't bad. And the view was pretty great. Mat showed me the various dials and gauges indicating the boat's speed, the wind speed and direction, the depth of the water. She pointed out where we were on the electronic charts, nautical maps which showed more detail about the seafloor than they did about the land. It was both simpler and more complicated than I'd imagined.

It seemed to take forever to approach the entrance to the bay. For the longest time it looked like we were aiming right at a cliff, but then suddenly I saw the opening to the bay, like one of those optical illusions where you can't see the picture at all until all of a sudden you do. "Sorry, Devi, but you'll have to move. We've got to do sail work soon."

"Sure." I scrambled up and discovered that it wasn't as hard to walk as I'd remembered. I still hung on to something as I went, but I got myself into the main salon and sat on one of the benches near a window to watch. The crew all appeared to know what to do as we sailed through a break in the rocks that seemed far too narrow, then turned left into a huge harbour.

There was nothing there — no town, no signs of

civilization at all, not even a fishing boat. It was like something out of a nature documentary. We sailed in for a few minutes, then in a flurry of activity and well-oiled gears the sails all disappeared. I heard a motor start and we slowly moved further into the bay. We turned into a small lobe off a beach and with a splash the anchor was down. A few revs of the engine later everything was quiet and I was joined by Mat and Christine.

"I'm afraid it's work time for you," Mat said. "We'll probably have to use the satellite link here since these hills block the nearby cell towers. If you need any help, I've asked Tulia to stand by. But you're kind of on your own, I'm afraid. Good luck."

I stood, revelling in the feeling of solidity under my feet. Time to see what was going on under the floorboards.

I couldn't sense the boat moving, but I made used all those handholds Isaac had pointed out anyway as I found my way to the server locker. While the laptop booted I took a closer look at the racks. It was a small configuration, which made sense, but I wondered how much business RRD could really be doing. Even with half a dozen nodes like this, the whole operation would barely be as big as a mid-size corporate data storage system. We weren't competing with Kim Dotcom, that was for sure. The blinkenlights were doing their thing, so power wasn't the issue. I figured with an electrician on board that wasn't likely, but I'd once wasted a day to finally notice that the box was unplugged so it was the first thing I checked now.

There was a text file on the laptop's desktop named "Manuel," which turned out to be a wiki-style combination of job log, notes on the system and missing tech manual. My predecessors had thankfully been diligent about keeping it updated, so I spent a while reading. I found the section on connecting to the satellite uplink and followed a few wires. I checked that I could locally access the system, which I could, so I guessed it wasn't a problem with the racks. Everything pointed to a connection error, which made sense since it was the flakiest part of the system. But it was also the part I didn't really understand.

I'd read up on satellite data transfer, but knowing how a thing works doesn't necessarily mean you know how to do a thing. Thankfully, I wasn't really on my own after all. I had Manuel. Surely between us we could get the system up and running in no time.

⚓

I was trying not to cry when I heard steps.

"I thought you might be hungry." It was Martin, with a large tupperware in one hand and a set of cutlery sticking out of his jeans pocket. I hadn't noticed until then, but I was, indeed, quite hungry.

"Thanks," I said, prying the lid off what turned out to be a big green salad with a generous helping of cooked fish. I speared a piece of fish and chewed. It was delicious. I managed to wait until I'd swallowed to ask what time it was.

"Around three," he said. "You've been down here a while." He looked at the servers and the glowing laptop. "Getting anywhere?"

I shook my head, my mouth full of salad. "The log files weren't self-deleting, so the disk filled up. Annoying but it happens. I fixed it and that should have been it, but I still can't get a connection. I don't know what the hell's going on." Martin had the deer-in-the headlights expression of someone who isn't following at all. "Sorry, just thinking out loud. What have you guys been up to?"

"Christine's doing yoga on the beach and a bunch of them went swimming, but I'm still waterlogged from the last few days at San Juan del Sur. Surfing — or pretending to, anyway. I spent most of my time flailing around underwater trying not to get hit in the head by my board."

"I've never tried."

"It's fun, but hard. I need a bit of rest. But we're going to be here a few days, so there's no rush to get the fun in." He frowned. "I hope you're not stuck down here the whole time. It's pretty nice out there. There's a little river you can get up in a kayak at high water, and sometimes you can see crocodiles in there."

"Are you serious?"

He nodded. "Snorkelling's pretty decent at this beach, too."

I sighed. A swim sounded really great just then and this bay seemed safe enough. "Don't make me jealous. I'm starting to think I'm going to be stuck down here forever."

He shrugged. "It sounds like all boat jobs — before you can even start to fix the thing that's broken you've got to do ten other things first just to get to it and one of them is in some locker you can't even get your whole arm into."

I stopped in mid-chew. "That's it!" I said around my lunch, then turned back to the laptop. The servers were fine now, but it was the connection that wasn't working. I remembered seeing something about one of the satellite cable's connections being housed in a tiny compartment under the workstation. "Can you help me with something?"

"Sure."

"Find me a screwdriver and a flashlight."

Martin disappeared around a corner and came back with a small toolkit. I unscrewed the base of the chair I'd been sitting on and we maneuvered it out of the way. I shone the light into the cavity that was revealed and could just make out a small electronics box tucked into a crevice. I turned off the light and saw the faint glow of an LED light. Yellow. Blinking three times.

"Gotcha!" I felt around for the reset button, nearly dislocating my shoulder in the process, but I got it eventually. No lights. A red light. Then blinking green. It seemed to blink for days but finally, miraculously, stayed on.

"Yes! You're a genius!" I grinned at Martin.

"You must have really needed that salad."

The sun on me felt great as I sat in the cockpit, revelling in my success. "I don't know why the satellite box barfed, but we are all systems go now."

I couldn't keep the grin off my face, even though I hadn't really done anything that impressive. If Martin hadn't mentioned things being crammed in tiny places, I don't know if I'd ever have thought to go look for the switch. But I still felt like I finally had a handle on being here.

"It could have happened weeks ago," Tulia said. "We've been using cell towers since we've been near shore, but there's no connection here. The satellite's probably been down since we had to reboot the power systems last month."

"Oh, yeah," Isaac said, "I forgot about that. Sorry, Devi. I should have mentioned it."

"We all knew," Tulia said. "It's just hard to remember how interconnected everything is sometimes."

"Well, it wasn't just the satellite," I said. "The log files clogging up the disk were messing things up, too." I could see their eyes glazing over, but I felt kind of like I had the first time I'd gotten a robot to walk across the floor unaided. I tried to rein in the tech talk.

"Glad to hear it," Mat said, appearing from around a bulkhead. She moved awfully quietly, I thought. "How about a beer? You deserve it."

"Uh..." I didn't want to sound ungrateful but the thought of drinking a beer turned my stomach. "I'm not really a beer person."

Mat shrugged. "Takes all kinds. Jimmy's got a little guava juice hiding in the reefer, and I'll authorize a rum ration if it's just beer you're not fond of."

I wasn't much of a drinker, but it felt like cause for celebration. I looked around and saw that most of the crew held beer cans encased in logoed cozies. "Sure, rum and juice sounds great."

Mat nodded and disappeared. "Good choice," Tulia said. "Mat doesn't play hostess often, so you should get while the getting's good. Besides, we're here to chill out for a few days — might as well make the most of it."

⚓

I'd never been a big reggae fan, but there is something magical about Bob Marley on the stereo when there's a rum drink in your hand and you're sitting on a boat in a tropical paradise. "This doesn't feel real," I said, listening to the animal sounds coming from the jungle. "You guys ever get used to it?"

"*Living the dream?*" Christine said, sarcasm rich in her voice. "Sure, on days like this it's all good times. But it's not a dream; it's real life and it's not always mai tais in a hammock."

"Do we even *have* a hammock?" Martin asked.

"Probably. But good luck finding it among all that computer stuff." It was obvious she didn't think much of the reason I was here. Or maybe it was just me she didn't like. If only I could go back to this morning and do something, anything, differently.

Jimmy's head popped up out of the doorway to the main salon. "What do you say to a barbecue on the back deck?"

"I say hell yeah," Christine said, her attitude adjusting instantly. "Any steak left?"

"A couple," he said, then turned to me. "Uh, do you eat meat?"

I nodded. "I'm not a Hindu; beef's okay. More of that fish from earlier would be great, too, if there aren't enough steaks."

"Oh, there will be plenty of fish, don't you worry." Jimmy chuckled and disappeared.

Martin produced a deck of cards and we played a few hands of gin rummy while Christine did some stretches on the foredeck before Jimmy returned with platters of bread, cheese and chopped veggies. After another trip down to the galley for supplies, Jimmy stood at the small propane grill poking the steaks with a fork. The smell was tantalizing.

I filled a plate and made my way over to the grill. "It's not a cheeseburger in paradise," Jimmy said as he put a slice of meat on my plate, "but it's close."

"Huh?"

"Be grateful you don't get the reference," Martin said. "You will soon enough."

I let it go, overwhelmed by the smell of dinner. I found a free space to sit and dug in.

⚓

I still hadn't gotten used to the fact that it was dark by seven pm. After dinner we'd drifted off to our separate activities, some reading and some watching a movie. Tulia went for another swim. I was tempted, but the idea of swimming in the ocean after dark seemed too much for my first real night aboard. And I found that even though it was still early, I was tired. I stuck it out as long as I could, but finally succumbed around nine.

I managed the curtains without incident and crawled into my bunk. Remembering the fan, I lay there for a moment, cooling off and trying to make sense of the day. So much had happened — my first sailing trip, finding my way around the server system. It somehow didn't seem so terrifying any more. I dropped off to sleep easily.

However, I woke in a panic.

I don't know how long I'd been asleep but there was a light brighter than seven suns shining through the window in the crew quarters. I'd thought the heavy curtains would block almost anything. Then I heard the voices. Unfamiliar men's voices speaking Spanish quickly and with authority. I knew I was being unfair and racist, but I couldn't help but remember stories of Mexican drug cartels and Nicaraguan death squads.

The curtains opened roughly and I squealed. It was Martin.

"It's okay," he said, his voice calm but serious. "It's the *Guardacosta*... the local coast guard. They just need to see everyone and they might take a look around to make sure we aren't carrying drugs. You'll have to come up."

"Okay," I said, but it didn't feel okay. It was the middle of the night and I wasn't even really sure where we were. I certainly was not up to being interrogated in a foreign language. I grabbed a tee shirt to throw over my flimsy tank top and followed Martin up to the main salon.

There were four men in uniform there, each holding a can of Coke or a beer, though none were drinking. Mat spoke with them in Spanish while Isaac handed them a series of papers. I recognized my passport among the documents, and heard Mat say my name. One of the men looked toward me, nodded, then went back to ignoring me.

This went on for a minute or two, then two of them went down below. They couldn't have been looking very hard for anything, because they were back in no time. "*Gracías, señora,*" one man said, then they filed out into the cockpit. I could see that there was a large open boat tied up alongside us with a massive spotlight aimed at the side of the *Byte Bucket*. That must have been what was shining in through the windows. The men boarded with their drinks, untied, and motored away.

The crew drifted off towards bed or whatever they were doing, but I was still shaking. As Isaac was putting the papers away I found my voice. "Is everything all right?"

He nodded. "We're barely over the border between Nicaragua and Costa Rica, and there's a little trafficking that goes on in this bay sometimes. They come by every few days to check it out, but they know us by now. They just have to fill out their paperwork and everything is okay."

"Well, I'm glad everything is in order."

He shrugged. "Well, technically, we *are* in the country illegally. But that's a different department, so these guys don't care. They just tell us to make sure to check in when we get to Cocos."

I was sure I'd heard him wrong. "What?"

At least he looked a bit sheepish. "It's not our usual procedure, don't worry. But the first port of entry is still a day away and the anchorage in here is too fantastic to pass up. They know it, we know it, and there's no easy way to get ashore here anyway so they just don't bother. Still, it's a bit nerve wracking whenever they come by. And they always do it after dark, too. Sorry you were startled."

I was more than startled, but what was there to say? Obviously the coast guard didn't mind us being there; the whole procedure had been more like a neighbourly visit than an official search. What could I do?

I went back to bed.

⚓

No one mentioned our nocturnal visitors the next day. I didn't feel like they were avoiding it or anything, more like no one cared. It bothered me, though. I kept reliving the incident — from the panic of being woken to the discomfort of seeing strangers on board. And the casual way that Isaac told me that we were essentially illegal aliens... I didn't like any of it, but what could I do about it? Maybe ignoring it was the right thing after all.

After breakfast I decided to try to have a good time. Martin showed me where the snorkel stuff was stored and I found a pair of flippers and a mask that kind of fit. "You dive?" he asked.

"Where I come from that water is freezing cold and black," I answered, marvelling at the clear turquoise water of the bay. "I've never even snorkelled before."

"Let me give you a few pointers." Martin showed me how to put soap in my mask to keep it from fogging, told me to wear a shirt over my swimsuit to avoid a sunburn, and reminded me to blow out the snorkel before trying to breathe. I must have looked like a Martian in all that mismatched gear, but once I slid into the warm water and got the hang of breathing through a tube, I forgot about everything.

It felt more like flying than swimming, floating on the top of the water, looking down at the world below. I'd never imagined there would be so many fish, especially near the rocks close to shore. Flashes of bright green, blue, and red made it hard to focus. I eventually settled on following a big spade-shaped fish with yellow and blue stripes. It barely noticed me at all as it swam from place to place around the rocks, nibbling at things. Other, smaller fish took off at its approach, but the larger fish were unconcerned. The underwater world was as serene as the picture on a postcard.

I'd never seen fish like this before. It had always

seemed to be such an unusual occurrence to see something in the water back home. Partially it was the murkiness, but also I think living in a city made it feel novel to see wildlife. The occasional sea lion was a cause for strangers on the street to talk to each other, pointing and snapping pictures. But mostly I suspect that we just didn't really look. Who has the time to peer into the water along the shore when you're living in the city? It was completely different here. It's not that there weren't things to do, but it wasn't pressing. I could stay down here as long as I wanted and I did. I swam around the small bay, entranced by the view of the bottom. It reminded me of the Vancouver Aquarium. The irony of that thought wasn't lost on me as I lazily paddled around the area.

Eventually, Martin swam up to me and gestured up. I popped my head out of the water and he said, "So? How's it going?"

"This is amazing."

He nodded. "We should probably think about heading back to the boat, though. It's easy to get sunstroke out here and you probably need some water." I must have given him a look, because he added, "Fresh water. To drink."

"Oh." Come to think of it, I was thirsty. I hadn't quite managed to avoid getting seawater in my mouth and the salt was intense. My lips felt like they were puckered. But I didn't want to leave. It was so quiet and beautiful under the water, I felt better than I had for as long as I could remember. I swam slowly back toward the boat, having to pop up and look around every few strokes. Looking at the universe under the water was disorienting and several times I found I'd turned myself around.

Back at the boat, Martin was already sitting on the side of the swim step. "Here, pass me your flippers."

I wrestled them off one at a time, careful not to drop them, and gave them to him. I hauled myself up and took off the rest of the snorkel gear. Martin passed me a bottle of water, which I gratefully drained. "Living the dream," I said.

"Yeah, today we are," he answered.

⚓

After lunch I checked on the servers to find them happily sending and receiving data, albeit at a rate much slower than I'd been accustomed to. Speed wasn't one of the things our customers were paying for, thankfully. I closed up the server room and wandered up to the front of the boat. Martin was lying in a hammock under a canvas shade someone had rigged up. There was an empty one nearby and I levered myself into it.

"You busy?" I asked.

"Do I look busy?" he answered with a grin. "And look — there were hammocks after all!"

"Yeah." I was quiet for a while, not knowing how to talk about what was on my mind. But it hadn't taken long after my swim for it to start bothering me again, and I knew that it would get worse if I didn't talk about it. I took a breath and kept my gaze on the trees on shore. "About last night..."

"Hmm?"

"Is that kind of thing, you know, common?"

"Getting boarded by the officials? Yeah, it happens once in a while. No biggie."

"I dunno," I said, "it seems like a big deal to me."

"Yeah, most places it doesn't happen after dark. That was unusual, but they do it at night out here because they want to catch the traffickers. They only boarded us because we were here and they had to once they saw us. They don't care about cruising boats."

"But we're here illegally." I hadn't meant to bring it up, but it came out of my mouth without thinking.

Martin didn't laugh at me, at least. "Yeah, I heard Isaac mention that. I don't know how it all works, but I'm pretty sure that's not common, either. We've been in and out of lots of countries since I've been on board and the captain has always been really strict about when we can and can't leave the boat. I know it doesn't seem like it right now, but she's a stickler for procedures ordinarily."

"Well, being in a country illegally doesn't sound like procedure to me."

He shrugged. "Sometimes local expectations are different in different places. They're crazy about paperwork in Mexico, but I guess Costa Rica is a bit more lax. Those guys last night didn't give a damn about whether we were checked in or not, so why should we?"

"It still seems wrong."

"Then go talk to Mat about it." He didn't sound like he was trying to get rid of me, just making a suggestion.

"She's cool, she'll tell you what she knows." At that, he pulled his ancient-looking bucket hat down over his eyes and the conversation was over.

⚓

I took one of the kayaks and went ashore. I sat on the beach looking out at the shark-faced *Byte Bucket* and feeling sorry for myself. I knew it was ridiculous — just that morning I'd been having the time of my life. But it seemed like this sort of thing kept happening to me. I was trying not to think about it, but I realized that this was all reminding me of my last robotics project. To everyone else's eyes it had been an unqualified success, but I felt like it was the lowest point of my academic life. Worse than when I failed fourth grade math.

It wasn't that we cheated. I'm pretty sure that I would have had the courage to say something if that had been the case. At least I like to think so. But as it was I didn't say anything. I didn't tell the organizers that the official rules that Robbie found deep in the departmental website were slightly different from the instructions all the teams have been given. I didn't tell them that, or that our entry had a distinct advantage because we chose to follow those guidelines. And the worst part was that I didn't even say anything to the team. I just smiled and went along with the group when Robbie, Janine, and Kris redesigned the unit with a larger power supply and a faster CPU.

I told myself that it would come out eventually, that I didn't need to rock the boat. But it never did. Even when I stood with them in front of all the other teams, a ribbon around my neck and our names being engraved on the trophy, I said nothing. Not to the professors, not to my teammates. I've still never told anyone about that. Just like I figured I wouldn't say anything about how much last night bothered me.

I saw movement on the deck of the *Bucket*; it looked like Jimmy waving his arms at me and I could almost make out shouting. Probably dinner time. I didn't want to go back, would rather have stayed on the beach and slept under a tree, but I needed to eat. And I didn't want to have to explain myself. So I waved back, got in the kayak, and paddled back to the boat.

I was on my third attempt to tie the kayak's rope to the two-horned cleat when a shadow crossed in front of me. I looked up and recognized Tulia blocking out the sun. I always thought of sailors as skinny guys with ropy arms, but Tulia was none of those things. I knew she was strong — I'd seen her hauling lines and cranking winches like it was nothing, but she was soft and round and beautiful. In another circumstance, it wouldn't be hard at all to develop a crush on someone like her. I didn't get the feeling she would be interested anyway, and the fact that she was looking at me like thunder helped cool any of those remaining thoughts.

"Sorry," I said, though I wasn't really sure what I'd done. "I can't seem to get this—" I looked down at the balled up string covering the cleat.

"Why not get Martin to do it?" Her voice was hard

and I thought recognized the sound of jealousy.

"If he were here I would." She frowned at me and looked around.

"Where is he?"

"Beats me," I said, the rope coming off the cleat again. "I've been ashore by myself all afternoon. Haven't seen him. Can *you* help me?"

She didn't move but something in her face changed. "Sure," she said, finally, kneeling down. She took the rope from me, and slowly wound it twice around the middle of the cleat, then wrapped it once across the top. "This is the tricky part," she said as she made a loop then turned it over on itself and slipped it over one of the horns. "See how it's caught under itself here, lying flat?" I nodded. "That locks it. Here, you try."

It took a few attempts, but I eventually got it. She nodded once then turned and walked away without saying anything else.

I sighed. The last thing I needed was one of the crew mad at me over something that wasn't even happening. But she hadn't accused me of anything, and I knew enough to know that coming out of nowhere to deny that there was something going on between Martin and me was the quickest way to make people think that we were a couple.

I put my stuff away then worked up the gut to track down Mat. I found her in the galley, getting a beer.

"Hey, captain, got a second?"

"Sure." She swung a leg over at bench and sat.

"What's on your mind?"

"So, about us being in the country illegally..."

She sighed and put the can down. "It's not an ideal situation, I know. And this is not our standard operating procedure, but it's one of those things everyone does and no one cares. It's just here and normally I wouldn't do it, but I really didn't want your first trip out to be an overnighter and we had to leave Nicaragua. Our visas had expired so I made a decision — I weighed all the options and chose the least bad one." She picked up her beer, but didn't drink.

"I hoped we'd miss the *Guardacosta* but what can you do? Sometimes you're unlucky. And they really don't give a crap about us. The cold drinks we gave them were the closest thing to a bribe they wanted and we probably didn't even have to do that." She took a sip and shrugged. "Besides, it's better we ran into them than the US Navy. Then things would get really interesting."

"How come? Why would they care where we are?"

"Oh, they don't care about where we are, they care about who we are," she said. "You know the US government is interested in what *Really Remote Desktop* does. If they boarded us it could get very annoying very quickly."

That was not something I'd really considered. I knew that RRD's business model earned them no friends among governments who wanted to track everything everyone does online — that was the whole point of the system. But I also knew that it was a legal operation, so there wasn't anything they could do, at least not within US borders. But in international waters...

I left Mat to her beer and went up above decks. This was a lot more complicated than I thought. I looked out over the small bay to the beach, its rocky shore glinting in the afternoon sunlight. I had a moment of panic as I realized that there was nowhere to go. I was stuck on a boat that was possibly a target for the US military, with half a dozen people I hardly knew.

What the hell was I thinking?

After another day of lounging on the beach, snorkelling, carefully avoiding both Martin and Tulia, and trying not to think about how uncomfortable I felt, the captain announced that we'd be going to Playas del Coco the next day. It was only a day's sail away, but we'd need an early start, so we all turned in before ten.

I had trouble sleeping again, tossing and turning in my bunk until I eventually gave up and put on my light to read. I was still making my way through *Cryptonomicon*. I wasn't a much of a fiction reader, and this was a doorstop, but I was enjoying it — if at a snail's pace. Who knows what time it was when I finally dropped off, but it must have been late because I completely slept through the crew raising the anchor.

I woke up mashed against the curtain, which luckily I'd secured the previous night to keep my light from bothering the others. I was a bit surprised to find that I wasn't panicking, even though it took me a while to figure out how to brace myself in the bunk while undoing the curtains. I escaped, got dressed and went up to the cockpit.

"Look who decided to come up for a visit," Christine said and I had a hard time convincing myself that she wasn't rolling her eyes.

"Hi," I said, sheepishly. "Sorry I slept in. Uh, you didn't need me for anything, did you?"

"You'd know it if we did," Isaac said from behind the wheel. "I'm just amazed you slept though us pulling up the anchor. It's not exactly quiet."

I shrugged. "Ear plugs."

"Ha," Martin said. "You *are* smart. It took me a month before I resorted to ear plugs."

"Enough chit chat," Mat said from around the side of the boat. "Martin, ready about."

"Aye, aye, ready," he said, his voice suddenly serious. I knew enough to get out of the way and zipped into the main salon. I watched as the crew performed their maneuvers and the sails switched from one side of the boat to the other. I nearly fell off the seat as the boat tipped over the opposite way. I guess I wasn't so smart after all.

Once I was sure we weren't about to do that again, I went down for breakfast. After, I went back above decks to watch the show. We passed by several bays that had a few boats in them and I saw people surfing close to shore. It was a lot more populated in this area, with small towns on the beach and fishing boats moving in and out. It dawned on me that we probably had cell service, so I picked my way down to the server locker. I found myself having to hang on in my seat as the boat swayed in the swell. I can't say I was actually seasick, but I sure didn't feel great.

As I poked through the setup menus I remembered what Mat had shown me about how the workstation could swing. I fumbled around for the mechanism and finally set the station free. As I sat there, it was a most unnerving, though much more comfortable, experience — it was as if the boat surged around me, but I was stable and secure in my seat. It didn't make me feel instantly better, but it stopped me from feeling any worse and I was able to switch the system from the slow satellite to the much better cell network. Once I was sure it was all running smoothly, I shut everything down and extricated myself from the workstation, securing it with the latches.

I lurched back up above decks, grateful for the fresh breeze outside. I got my PFD — the inflatable life jacket harness — and found a secure spot out of the way. After a while I started to feel more human and when Jimmy came up with sandwiches, I was happy to take one.

⚓

I'd been surprised at how touristy San Juan del Sur had been, but Playas del Coco was in another league. Fancy resorts, huge American-style supermarkets, souvenir stands. We'd anchored out in the bay just before sunset, and had a quiet night on board. The next morning, Mat asked everyone to load into the dinghy to go ashore so we could check in. I still found it hard to get in and out of the inflatable, but at least I didn't fall out. Isaac piloted us to the beach and we all hauled on the boat to pull it up on shore.

"Is it safe to just leave it here?" I asked as we started walking up the beach.

"Sometimes stuff gets stolen," Isaac said, "but they won't get far rowing." He lifted his arm to show off a brightly-coloured bracelet with a thing that looked kind of like a bobby pin hanging from it. "Engine cut-off," he explained.

I was about to ask how it worked when a terrifying noise rang out overhead. It was like something from a horror movie and I discovered that not only was I rooted to the spot, I'd also grabbed Martin's arm and was squeezing him half to death. "What was that?"

"Howler monkeys," Martin said, prying my fingers out of his flesh and pointing up. "Watch out — they sometimes throw... stuff."

"What kind of stu— Oh." I remembered what monkeys do and picked up the pace to get out from under their tree. I caught Tulia's eye and it was pretty obvious she'd seen me grab Martin. She did not look happy.

Another howl from the tree dragged me out of my thoughts. "Wait 'til we're out at anchor somewhere calm and quiet and then they start up. It's like something from a Tarzan movie."

I shook my head. "How am I ever going to get used to all this?"

"You're only been aboard a few days, Devi. You're doing fine. And don't forget, this is supposed to be new and exciting — everything being weird is part of the point."

We walked into town and trooped into an office with an anchor on the door and a sign reading *Capitanía del Puerto*. Mat and the woman behind the counter exchanged some words in Spanish and Mat handed over a stack of papers and pointed at us. The woman behind the counter barely looked at us then waved her hand dismissively, saying something to Mat. The captain turned toward us and said, "You can all go. Enjoy the town. I'll probably be here all day with the officials. Isaac, turn on your phone and I'll call you when I need to get back to the boat."

"Will do," Isaac said. "Okay, why don't we say you all have a few hours ashore and then I'll be taking the dinghy back to the boat. Meet you at the beach at—" he looked at his wristwatch, "let's say two pm."

"You want a hand at the supermarket?" Tulia asked Jimmy after shooting daggers at me and Martin. Jimmy didn't seem to notice and just nodded, then they set off inland.

"I'm getting a burger and a beer," Isaac said and Christine's eyes lit up.

"Count me in," she said, "how about you guys?"

"I'm not really hungry," I said, though I didn't know how I was going to fill four hours in a strange town all alone.

"Me neither," Martin said. "Wanna go for a walk?"

"Sure."

Isaac and Christine shared a glance, but Isaac just said, "Okay, see you later." They walked away and I stood there for a moment not knowing what to do now.

"Let's go," Martin said, and we set out walking.

We wandered up and down the main street of the town, looking at the shops and restaurants. It was good to stretch my legs; I hadn't realized how cooped up I was feeling on the boat. I didn't know how to tell him about Tulia and at that moment I didn't really care. It was just so nice to have someone to talk to, even if it was about nothing.

"So how did you end up on the *Byte Bucket?*" I asked.

"Accident, really," Martin said. "I was backpacking in Mexico with my girlfriend. Ex-girlfriend, now. It was her idea, go have some grand romantic adventure. It turned out to be more hard work and less romance than either of us expected. Long story short, we broke up in Zihuatanejo and she was the one paying for everything. I was stuck when she left. I met this guy at the hostel who said that you can sometimes get on as crew with the sailing boats that come through, and it can be a way back up north, so I started hanging around the cruising club. I was pretty broke when the Bucket pulled in, but they were the only boat around that needed crew. I knew they weren't headed north right away, but I was down to my last few pesos. It was get on the boat or go hungry, so I got on the boat. I've just about got enough saved up to get home, so this is the last leg I'll be on."

I felt my stomach drop. I don't know why I'd assumed that everyone was going to be there for the whole term I'd be aboard, but I had. The idea of Martin leaving bothered me. Regardless of whatever Tulia might think, I certainly didn't have a crush on him, but he was the closest thing to a real friend I had here. I didn't want to lose that. Still, I understood about wanting to go home.

"Good for you," I said with as much enthusiasm as I could muster. "That must have been scary, being stuck in a foreign country, not knowing how you'll get home. Couldn't you have called your parents or something?"

"My parents died in a car crash a few years ago," he said without emotion.

"Oh, god, Martin, I'm sorry. I can't believe I just said that." I wished one of those howler monkeys would throw something at me — I'd have rather been covered in monkey shit than feel like such a jerk.

Martin was cool about it, though. "It's all right, you didn't know. That's part of why I let Rachel talk me into the Mexico trip. I guess I was kind of messed up after they died — I took a year off from University and never quite made it back. I didn't know what I was doing, still don't really. But being on the boat gave me some order. Having someone tell me what to do was exactly what I needed, I think. But I can't stay out here forever. It's time to go home."

"Yeah," I said. "I know what you mean."

"How did you pick this gig?" he asked. "With a name like yours I guess you must have always heard the call of the sea."

I laughed. "Not really. I can't say I got here by accident, too, but that's kind of what it feels like. I applied for a bunch of co-op jobs, same as everyone else in my program. I didn't particularly want this one and honestly didn't fully understand what I was getting into when I put in my application. It was just on the list, so I applied. Then when the offer came, all of a sudden everyone around me is talking about how great this opportunity is, how I'd be an idiot to pass it up. My parents, my profs, everyone." I stopped in front of a roadside shop selling trinkets and picked up a small embroidered bag. Jeannette would have loved it. "I haven't told anyone this, but if it were up to me I'd have picked the other offer I got. A boring, safe, ordinary office job."

"It *was* up to you, though," Martin said, "wasn't it?"

"Technically," I said, "but how could I disappoint everyone? Even my girlfriend—" I felt my face getting hot. I hadn't meant to talk about any of this with anyone, but I couldn't stop myself. "Even Jeannette, who didn't want me to go, even she said I'd be dumb not to take it. Then she broke up with me. After that what choice did I really have?" I sat down on a bench at the edge of the each and stared out at the boats at anchor.

"Well," Martin said after a moment, "as much as I'm happy you're here, I think they were kind of jerks to railroad you into doing something you didn't want to do. I mean, who does that? If you tell people you don't want to do something, they should accept that. After all, it's your life."

"Yeah," I said miserably. "I never exactly said I didn't want to go."

"Oh."

"I didn't want to disappoint anyone and they were all so excited for me." I shrugged. "Besides, it's not all bad." I jumped slightly as the local howler monkeys started up their song. "At least they aren't throwing shit."

Martin grinned. "Yet."

⚓

The simplest things become a lot more complicated when you're doing them on a boat. Tulia and Jimmy arrived at the beach laden down with shopping bags and I eyed the ratio between passengers and cargo and the space in our inflatable. It didn't look good, but they just started loading up the boat. I went to get in, but Isaac stopped me.

"We've got to push the boat out past the surf." I followed his line of sight about a meter out where the small waves were breaking as they neared shore. "We'll jump in there."

I looked over at Martin who just shrugged, then took off his flip flops and threw them in the dinghy. I noticed then that most of the crew wore rugged hiking sandals that had obviously been used for wading. I looked down at my own Birkenstocks, wondering whether they or my feet would come out worse. I decided to chance going barefoot; they were my only sandals.

I stuffed my shoes into my little backpack and took up a position on the side of the boat as we eased it out into the surf. The sand was soft, at least, though I ended up getting the bottoms of my shorts wet as we waded out until the water was up past my knees. "Okay, everyone in."

I gracelessly clambered into the boat over the side, and watched as Isaac threw himself against the back of the boat, levering his body in as the momentum gave us all one last push into deeper water. He quickly got the motor down and started and then we were off. It was slower going than on the way out because of all the extra weight, but it still didn't take long before we were back on board the *Bucket*.

I helped carry the haul down to the galley and heard Jimmy say to Isaac, "I ran into Frankie and Susan at the store. I thought we'd have them over tonight, if you think Mat won't mind."

"We aren't leaving the area for a few days," Isaac answered, "I'm sure a boat party tonight will be fine. Though if Mat's back early enough, we might head over to Huevos today."

Jimmy nodded and began stowing items. There were storage areas all over the place; under seats, behind cushions, even in the floor. "I told those guys we'd hail them on seven-two; we can let them know where we'll be." Isaac nodded and went off toward his quarters.

I helped Jimmy put the last of the food away then went up above decks. I'd found a spot of shade on the foredeck and was making another dent in *Cryptonomicon* when I heard hushed voices. I don't know why it is that I have no trouble ignoring other people when they're talking normally, but as soon as I hear whispers, I can't help by try to make out what they're saying.

I was sure one of them was Martin, but I couldn't tell who he was talking to.

"...but I'm *not* a sailor," he was saying, "I'm just a guy

who ran out of money and took the only way out he could find. I never wanted to sail off into the sunset, I just wanted to make enough to get home."

The other voice was muffled and harder to hear, so I had to strain to listen. I knew I should have given them some privacy, but I couldn't help myself. "What do you have to go home to, anyway? Some crummy McJob while you figure out your life?"

"It's not like I'm making mad stacks out here."

"You already made enough to get back home." Their voices were getting a bit louder, either because they were getting angry or because they were getting closer. Either way, I picked up my book to make it look like I was reading. "At least here you don't have to pay for room and board, and you can feel sorry for yourself on the boat just as well as you can in some crappy basement apartment."

"Have you ever thought that maybe I *want* to live in a crappy basement apartment? Maybe what I want is a nice, normal, stable life where I wake up in the same place every day, and I never have to wonder how long it will be before I see Corn Flakes again."

"We have lots of Corn Flakes."

"That's not the point and you know it. Besides, why do you care what I do? You just don't want to have to break in another deck hand."

Whoever it was laughed, but it didn't sound like anything was particularly funny. "This isn't about me, man. I just don't want to see you throwing away the opportunity of a lifetime. But if you really want to go back, go back. No one is making you stay. Just think about this: when you've gotten everything you want — the career, the mortgage, the two point five kids — when you're sitting in front of the TV for the umpty-millionth night in a row, do you think you might wonder what might have been if you'd said yes just once instead of taking the easy way out? Just think about it, okay?"

"You don't know anything about me." I could hear him stomp away, then the door to the main salon slammed. I turned a couple of pages as Christine came into view.

"Oh, jeez," she said as she saw me. "I didn't realize you were here."

"Just doing a little reading," I said, holding up the book as evidence. "Uh, you have a nice lunch ashore?"

"What? Oh, yeah, I did, thanks." She gave me a look, and I figured she must know that I'd overheard her conversation with Martin. She didn't say anything else, though, and I certainly wasn't going to bring it up. She tidied a few of the ropes on the deck then gave me a curt nod and headed toward the back of the boat.

I wondered what that was all about, but it wasn't really any of my business. Poor guy. I knew what it was like to have everyone around you telling you what to do. Of course, I didn't want to him to leave, either.

The captain returned late in the afternoon, with the paperwork all settled. I'd heard a familiar noise that I couldn't place, when I saw Isaac take an old flip phone from his pocket, talk for a moment, then jump in the dinghy and speed to shore.

Of course, we had cell service here. It occurred to me that I hadn't been in contact with anyone since San Juan del Sur. It had only been five days but it felt like a lifetime. I went down to my bunk and pulled my phone out from the ziplock baggie where I'd stashed it. It started up, and I made a note to myself to plug it in the next time I was down in the server locker. It took forever to get a signal, but when it did I got four bars and a seemingly endless stream of texts.

Several from both my mom and dad, a couple of roaming notifications from the phone company, and two from Jeannette. Two. I couldn't understand why she'd text me at all, let alone twice. I sat on the side of my bunk and pulled up the ones from my dad first. He wanted to know everything about the boat, and the crew, and where we were, then demanded photos several times. Mom was a bit more reserved; it didn't sound like she was worried, exactly, but I sent back a quick text to them both.

> On the boat in Costa Rica!
> Everyone's cool the servers are
> running it's beautiful here. There
> are monkeys! No pics yet, sorry.
> Love you miss you!!

I already knew that personal use of the internet on board was fairly restricted. We had a good connection, but we paid for every byte, so the crew was limited to sending one text-only email a week, and we were expected to go ashore for getting messages and anything else. I prepped a longer message on my phone's notepad using the small Bluetooth keyboard I'd brought and reminded myself to get some pictures. I wished I'd been more prepared when we'd gone ashore — several of the restaurants in Coco advertised wifi.

After that was done I couldn't come up with another reason to put it off any longer and opened up my texts again. Jeannette.

```
hi just wanted to see how you are
and hope you're having the
adventure of a lifetime you're the
awesomest wish I was there!! <3 J
```

Okay. Well that was random. It's not like we had a bad break-up but she did dump me. We had only been together a few months, and it wasn't like we were picking out china patterns or anything. Neither of us had even said the L word. But I really liked her, and it hurt when she told me she thought we should break up. She wasn't ready for a long-distance relationship, and didn't want to be the reason I gave up this opportunity. She didn't even come to my good-bye party. So why was she trying to talk to me now, when I was on a boat thousands of miles away. It's not like I could do anything about it now. Did she really miss me?

Her next message was time-stamped the next day.

```
sorry for the drunk text too many
sambuca shots at the bowl you are
the coolest tho
```

I sighed. It was a kind of explanation, I supposed. My thumb hovered over the delete icon, but I couldn't quite bring myself to dump the messages. I was still staring at the screen when I heard someone come into the bunk room.

"Hey, you okay?" It was Christine. "It's freaking gorgeous out there and you're holed up in here. Everything all right?"

"Yeah," I said, turning the connection off on my phone and stuffing it in my pocket. "I just realized I hadn't let my folks know that I haven't drowned. Yet."

She laughed. "Yeah, it's good to keep the landlubbers in the loop. Their imaginations can run away with them. I blame *The Perfect Storm*." I made a face, but she just kept talking. "We're about to move the boat around the corner. It's really nice over there; a quiet beach, great snorkelling, fishing if you like that kind of thing. You should come up."

"Okay." This was the first friendly conversation we'd had so I followed her up above decks and watched the anchoring procedure. It was amazing the amount of communication they could do with just hand gestures. Soon we were motoring away from Coco and rounding the rocks off the point. The next bay was large, with several smaller bays along the shore. We pulled into the small cove around the point, and anchored just off the beach. Once we were settled I could hear the screams I now easily identified as howler monkeys. I pulled out my phone and took a series of snaps: the beach, the boat, the bay. That ought to keep my dad happy for a while, if I ever got around to sending them to him.

Mat, Jimmy, and Christine took off in the dinghy to go fishing, and I fumbled with a hammock on the foredeck. I'd just gotten in when Martin appeared. "Mind if I hang out here?"

"Sure," I said. I didn't want to bring up the conversation I'd overheard, or Tulia's weirdness, but felt like they were hanging between us. "How's it going?"

He shrugged. "It's going." He didn't seem inclined to say any more, so I didn't push it. What was I going to say? *I was eavesdropping and I know you're unhappy and I don't have any useful advice but want you to tell me about it anyway?* No, thanks.

"So," I began, searching for something safe to talk about, "I heard something about a party tonight. Is that happening?"

He nodded. "I guess there's a boat at Coco that the rest of them all know. Happens all the time in busy harbours, running into people you know. Socializing is a major part of the boat life." He looked thoughtful. "I think it's kind of like the way they buy stuff; if you see something you want, you better get it because you never know if you'll find it at the next port. Same thing with friends. If they're around, better hang out now because you never know if you'll see them again."

I took that in. "That sounds horrible. How depressing."

He shrugged. "It's what happens when you're on the move. People come and go, you see them when you do and make the most of it. It's tough, but it's got its good side, too. You'll see. It's not so bad out here."

I wondered who he was trying to convince, me or himself.

⚓

From my vantage point in the hammock, I watched the small rowboat approaching from across the bay. It wasn't a huge distance in our dinghy with its powerful motor; the gang out fishing had been over to the other side and back several times that afternoon. But it looked like slow going in the rowboat. I could make out two people in the boat and guessed that they were our visitors. I marked my place in my book then went to the back of the boat to see who was around. I saw Mat poring over some paper charts and cleared my throat.

"Looks like visitors, Captain." She looked off into the distance, then grinned.

"Excellent! Jimmy," she hollered. "Company's coming!"

I heard a muffled response from down below, but the rest of the crew appeared on deck.

"Is that *S Cargo*?" Christine asked, squinting at the approaching rowboat.

"Yeah, we ran into them at the store," Tulia said.

"Man, I can't remember the last time I saw them. La Paz, maybe?"

"Nah, we crossed paths in El Salvador for a few days," Mat said. "They left just after we got there."

"That's right!" Tulia said. "I'd almost forgotten about that party we had when we arrived. Must have been a hundred people aboard that night."

"A hundred people?" I couldn't imagine twenty people aboard the *Bucket*, let alone a hundred.

"Yeah, that was some night," Isaac said. "I was a little worried about our waterline."

The rowboat bumped into the stern and Mat went down to meet the guests. She took a couple of loaded cloth bags from them and handed them up to Isaac. He took them away as Mat helped the two people aboard.

I put them in their mid-thirties, his hair long and free-flowing, hers almost a buzz cut. They both wore shorts and tank tops and no shoes. When they got out of their little boat, they took turns hugging Mat then climbed aboard. There were more hugs and cheek kisses, then they got to me.

"Ah, the new crew member," the guy said. "I'm François, this is Susan. Nice to meet you." He had a Québecois accent and a disarming grin.

"Hi, I'm Devi." I lifted a hand in a weak wave, vaguely uncomfortable with the affectionate displays going on. No one tried to hug me, though, so that was good at least.

"How long have you been aboard, Devi?" Susan

asked.

"Uh, like five days."

She laughed. "Well, you're in good hands," she leaned in and half-whispered, "even if it doesn't seem like it."

"I heard that," Isaac said coming back out on deck and Susan laughed. "Come on, let's see what goodies you brought for us."

We trooped into the main salon, where Jimmy had set out a good selection of snacks. Chips, bread, crackers, cheese, a few homemade-looking dips. There was a cooler filled with ice and beer, and there were a few bottles of liquor out as well. I wondered if I was finally going to see some drunken sailors. Until now, the crew tended to have a beer or two in the evenings and that was it.

We found seats and plates of food and they started catching up.

"So, where have you been since El Salvador?"

"We got an actual contract," Susan said, "so we had to bash up the coast back to La Cruz."

"How was the Tehuantepec?"

"We went way offshore, so it was okay, but it added a day or so to the trip. Still, it was good to actually have money coming in for a change. How was your crossing?"

"We motored the whole way," Martin said, then he must have caught the baffled look on my face. "Oh, sorry, Devi. The Tehuantepec is this huge bay between Mexico and Guatemala. Apparently the wind there gets really ridiculous, but it was dead calm when we were there." He shrugged as if he didn't really believe there was anything to be concerned about.

"It can be really dangerous," Isaac said, "it's either calm or horrible. I know of a few boats who rolled out there." He turned to François. "So what was this gig you got?"

"An actual shipping job, if you can believe it." He explained that they were trying to help pay for the costs of sailing by offering their services as an environmentally friendly shipping company. "*S Cargo*, shipping at a sail's pace."

"It started as a joke," Susan said. "When we first talked about going cruising we were trying to figure out how we could afford it. Then we ended up naming the boat *S Cargo*, because you know, sailboats are about as fast as a speedy snail."

"In our case," François broke in, "it's not that speedy."

Susan rolled her eyes good-naturedly and went on. "Then we thought, why not try and see if we could get some business? It's not like we're on some kind of schedule here. We don't really care where we go, we just want to be out on the water. And we finally got a contract."

"What was it?"

"An expat-American crafter living in Golfito who makes pretty cool stuff out of driftwood and other found items from the beaches. He's a real artist and the marina up in La Cruz wanted to have some in their shop. We'd been hanging out with Marco, the guy who makes the stuff, and he's big into sustainability."

"It took a lot longer than if he'd just used FedEx," François said, "but he gets to say that the whole process of his product is environmentally friendly, so it was worth it to him. And it's keeping us in chick peas, so we're happy."

"Well, who are we to say that you've got a crazy business model?" Mat said. "RRD isn't exactly doing the standard thing, either." She turned to me. "Of course, it means we get to work with these computer geniuses who want to do cutting edge stuff."

She didn't sound like she was making fun of me and no one was laughing. I smiled and mumbled something about how it was still early days. Thankfully, François took that moment to ask for another drink and I fled to the food table.

I'd loaded my plate with an assortment of snacks when I heard a loud boom.

"Shit," Isaac said, peering out the door. "Thunderstorm."

The crew leapt up, each of them headed in a different direction. "Give me your phone," Christine said to me, holding out her hand.

"Okay," I dug it out of my pocket. "Why?"

"I'm putting all the handheld electronics in the oven in case we get hit by lightning." She grabbed a few more small items, then took off down below.

Hit by lightning? That couldn't possibly... Oh shit.

The servers.

⚓

I ran down to the server locker, trying to figure out what to do. I understood Christine's plan: the oven would act as a Faraday cage, protecting the electronics from getting fried in case of a lightning strike. But I could live without my phone a lot easier than we could live without all the electronics down in the locker. And they weren't exactly going to fit in the oven, even if I could disconnect them all in time.

I looked around, seeing the space in a different light. The laptop was sitting out on the workstation, but it was easily movable. I powered it down and disconnected it from the rest of the system. I followed a few wires and saw that the cupboard where the racks were installed wasn't like the other storage areas on board.

Most of the cupboards and cabinets were made of a combination of plywood and fibreglass, but the server racks were metal. I stuck my head all the way in the cabinet, shining a flashlight all around. The whole structure was a metal lattice, and I could just make out that the metal extended even to the backs of the sliding doors which could be closed. The whole compartment was shielded. I sighed with relief, found a spot to tuck the laptop and closed the doors, securing them with a latch.

I should have known that I wouldn't be the first person to have this thought. Still, I found that my heart was pounding. It didn't get any better when a deafening crash sounded.

I'd never heard lightning so close before and all I could think of was the aluminum mast soaring up above us. If ever there was a more obvious lightning rod, I didn't know what it was. I noticed for the first time the screws in the floor — metal screws that would conduct electricity much better than the wood parquet. I wished I were wearing shoes, though wondered if that would even make a difference.

I carefully walked to the ladder, avoiding the screw heads as much as possible. The ladders' rungs were wood, but I climbed as quickly as possible. I wasn't sure if being above decks was better than being below, but I didn't want to be alone. What did you do on a boat if you got hit by lightning anyway?

Rain pounded down, so loud that it was hard to talk. Even so, it was apparent that I wasn't the only one who was scared. Lightning exploded in the sky, momentarily blinding me, and a terrible cracking sound shook the boat at nearly the same time. "Fuck!" It was Isaac. I'd never heard him shout, never even imagined his demeanour to escalate beyond pretty chill.

"It'll be over soon." Mat's voice was calmer than Isaac's, but even she sounded rattled. "At least we're catching lots of rain." I followed her pointed finger to see a torrent of water spilling from the canvas cover stretched over part of the cockpit. I'd wondered why it was in such a strange configuration, but now I understood. Rain water pooled in the edges, then ran down hoses attached to the steel support bars and into what I assumed were tanks.

She was right, though; the storm passed quickly. The rain soon petered out and the booming sounds faded off into the distance. Before I'd even had time to really contemplate what was happening, the sun came out again.

"Well, that was more exciting than I'd planned," Mat said. "Who wants a beer?"

⚓

François and Susan stayed another few hours, telling stories about unfortunate boats that had been hit by lightning. Apparently, one could expect anything from a few scorch marks to a hole in the hull. No wonder they were all nervous. "I hate lightning," Isaac said, more than once. "It's the worst part about Central America."

"How often do storms like that happen?" I asked.

"At this time of year, once a week or so," Mat answered. "Getting less often. But a few months ago it was almost every afternoon."

Isaac shivered and popped another beer.

"We'll be sailing away from this weather, though," Tulia said. "Once we get south of the equator it's not lightning we'll have to deal with as much as the ITCZ."

"The what?"

"The inter-tropical convergence zone. The doldrums."

"What does that mean?" I'd heard of doldrums before, but I didn't see how being bored was as challenging as lightning storms.

"There's no wind," Isaac said. "No wind means no sailing which means you can get stuck there. Just sitting there, day after day, going nowhere."

"Or going backwards," François said, an evil grin on his face. "I know of a boat that took over fifty days to cross the Pacific, and spent a week making negative miles."

"Well, I'm here to make sure that doesn't happen," Christine said. "We don't like to motor for distance if we can help it, but we're not spending any time going backwards."

"Wait a minute," I said. "Are we going to be crossing the Pacific... now?" I didn't want to sound terrified, even though I was.

"Nah," Mat said. "Not yet. We're just going to the Galápagos."

The what? Geography wasn't my best subject in school but even I knew that the Galápagos was among the most remote places on the planet. That was the whole point of Darwin's journey — to investigate all the unusual animals that had evolved in isolation.

"Uh, how long will that take?"

Mat shrugged. "A week, probably less. It's about time we put out to sea again. I'm getting restless with all this time in port."

"Boats aren't made for the harbour," Susan agreed and turned to me. "This is so exciting for you — your first passage! And what a place to make landfall. You're going to love it there."

I think I said something sensible, but all I could think of was lightning, the boat rocking all day every day for a week, being out of sight of land on our way to the middle of nowhere. Maybe Mat was kidding. Surely we wouldn't be leaving the safety of shore so soon.

I hadn't even been on the boat for a week.

We stayed in the area for three more days: the *Byte Bucket* at anchor in Bahía Huevos and Isaac taking whoever needed to go ashore in the dinghy. He made several runs every day to Coco when we needed things and it seemed that we needed all the things.

The day after the lightning storm, I spent a few hours at one of the local restaurants, enjoying the local breakfast dish of rice and fried eggs called *pinto gallo* and using their wifi. I'd have felt guilty taking up a table with my phone and keyboard, except that the place was full of backpackers doing the same thing. Half the tables had people with headphones and laptops, Skyping with someone.

I sent a long email to my parents, with all the photos I'd taken and news of our upcoming passage. I played up the "OMG, I'm going to the Galápagos" angle and minimized the "holy shit, I'm going to be in the middle of the ocean on a glorified raft" aspect of the trip. My parents were obviously supportive of what I was doing — too supportive, I was thinking now. But I couldn't help remembering what Christine had said about folks back home assuming that it was all *The Perfect Storm* out here, and I knew my parents well enough to know that they'd try to keep their concerns to themselves for my sake. So I kept it light.

I sent a different, more honest email to my brother.

Hey, Nico.

So I guess I'm off to the Galápagos now. I should be excited but it's kind of terrifying. We are going to be sailing for almost a week without stopping! People really do this?

The crew totally know their stuff. Christine (mechanic) is in the engine room all day, every day, making sure everything is cool with the motor. The captain is busy plotting our course and studying the weather. You would not believe how much we talk about the weather. I wouldn't be surprised if they pray to the Wind God.

I think we have bought out every food store in Coco — we're anchored in a bay off this cute little tourist town in Costa Rica. It's all so weird — we have to take a little boat in to the beach every day. I can't believe no one has stolen it. Anyway, the amount of food they're laying in makes me think we'll be at sea for a month. Martin and Tulia, the two deckhands, are busy squaring the boat away — stowing things in lockers, wrapping breakables in towels, inspecting lines and the rest of the rigging.

They all obviously know what they are doing, but holy shit, bro — the Galápagos? I'm sure once I stop freaking out it's going to be awesome. It's going to be awesome, right?

I won't be able to email again
until we get there. Here's some
pics. Don't worry, I'll be doing
enough worrying for us both.

Love,
Devi
PS. Don't tell mom and dad about
the freaking out part.

As I wrote to Nico, I realized how much of the lingo I'd picked up. I still felt like they were speaking a foreign language half the time, but it was getting better. Maybe by the time we got to the Galápagos, I'd be able to tell the difference between port and starboard.

⚓

The morning of our departure, I rowed ashore to the small beach nearby with Christine. We hadn't become friends but at least now we were talking without venom. We weren't intending to hang out: she wanted one last yoga session on terra firma and I just wanted terra firma. I left her to her downward dog and walked over to the rocks at the edge of the peninsula. There was a hole in the rock that had been worn by the waves. When the tide was high, water surged through there, making an eerie sound. At low water, you could see through the hole to the main bay by Playas del Coco. A more adventuresome person could probably pick their way through the rock, but I was content just to observe.

You could see where the years of erosion had marked the stone, smooth and rippled in places. It always amazed me how something so seemingly unyielding could be transformed over time. I understood the mechanics behind the process, but it was still slightly shocking. The world always appeared immutable to me; not just the physical landscape, but people and systems. Obviously things changed — here I was, miles away from home, my everyday life as different from what it was only a few weeks ago as I could imagine — but I was fundamentally the same. I would always be the same; everyone is who they are and where people get into trouble is when they try to force themselves to change. Or worse, try to change someone else.

The leopard can't change its spots, right?

But standing there on that beach, watching the ebb and flow of the ocean through what had obviously once been a solid wall of stone, I wondered if I might be wrong. What if life is like water? What if all of our experiences and choices are like those ocean waves, each one seeming to make no impact but over time they shape us into entirely different people than we were before? What if we can become the people we wish we could be?

⚓

I'd been thinking about how to manage the servers while we were at sea. It wouldn't take long before we were out of cell range, even with our own tower, so we'd be relying on the satellite link. I wasn't confident in its performance, and I was really not confident in my ability to troubleshoot. Still, that was the one area of the voyage where I had any experience, so I found that I couldn't stop thinking about it.

We weighed anchor shortly after noon and the crew raised the mainsail before we'd even left the bay. It didn't seem very windy to me, and it looked like Martin and Tulia were doing a lot more on the foredeck than they had on the previous voyages. I kept out of the way on the aft deck and watched as not one but two sails were unfurled at the bow. It felt like something out of a pirate movie, even though I knew the Bucket was a modern sailboat. There was just something magical about being pulled along by all those white billowing sails. It made me forget to be nervous.

We spent the afternoon sailing away from shore and as I watched the land recede behind us there was a part of my brain that knew I should be freaking out, but I felt totally calm. I was even starting to get used to walking around the boat while it rolled lazily in the waves.

I ran into Mat as I was on my way out of the head. "Hey, Devi, how are you doing so far?"

"Pretty good." I grinned at her. "I was just going to go down and check on the system."

She nodded. "You might want to keep your trips down into the hold pretty short to start. If you're going to get seasick, it'll be at the beginning of the trip and it'll be way worse down there. If you start feeling bad, come up above decks and get some fresh air. And let me or Isaac know, okay?"

"Sure." I'd forgotten about seasickness. I thought I felt okay, but worry started to creep back into my consciousness.

"Oh, and Jimmy's going to have supper ready earlier than usual when we're under way so the off watch crew can get to bed earlier."

"Right. Um, what hours am I supposed to be keeping?"

She shrugged. "Whatever you want. You're not crew, so you don't have a watch. If you'd rather be up all night and sleep during the day, that's fine with me, so long as you keep the system up."

"Okay, thanks." She nodded and went back up to the cockpit. I was intrigued by the idea of night watch. I'd been a night owl when I was younger, but early morning classes at university had painfully broken me of that habit. I decided to spend the next week trying to just follow my body's natural rhythms — sleep when I was tired, work when I was awake, eat when I was hungry. It was appealing, but as I carefully made my way down to the server room, I realized that there was very little natural about my current situation. Still, it would be interesting.

I unhooked the workstation and set it swinging, then climbed in. Everything was running fine with decent throughput, though we were still getting a cell signal. Things would be different later, I knew. I noticed that there was a patch available for one of our logging programs. That would have to wait until we were somewhere more stable — the Galápagos, I guessed. I set the system to ignore the upgrade for now and gave everything a last check. I'd have to reconfigure the network the next day, but for now it looked like I was free to enjoy the trip. So I carefully stowed my equipment and then locked the workstation back in place. As I weaved back to the ladder, I noticed that I felt a bit strange in the stomach, though not as bad as the last time I'd been down here when we'd been under way. So far, so good.

⚓

Dinner was light, but tasty, and I found that I wasn't as hungry as I usually was at suppertime. Jimmy knew his business. We all ate together in the cockpit, Isaac uncharacteristically dominating the conversation.

"I was seven when I made my first ocean passage." He looked wistful as he stared out to sea. "We'd been living on the boat for as long as I could remember, but the longest we'd ever been at sea was an overnighter. With two little kids, I think my parents were concerned about how they could handle both of us plus the boat. But by the time I was seven my sister was five, and I guess they both thought that was old enough."

"Did the two of you actually help with the sailing?" I asked.

"Not really," he said. "They let me haul the odd sheet once in a while and I took the wheel plenty. But mostly my sister and I read books and failed to catch fish and went skiing when it was rough."

"Skiing?" Christine cocked an eyebrow.

"Yeah, it's kind of ridiculous thinking back on it. When we'd get into the big swells, you know, and the boat's rolling from side to side like crazy, we'd put on a pair of wooly socks and slide around on the cabin floor, like we were skiing. It was so much fun, and got us out of our parents' hair, which meant they could concentrate on sailing."

"I can't imagine cruising with kids," Mat said. "Sure, most of the time you're just sitting around watching the ocean go by, but when shit happens — it *happens*. You can't be dealing with a tantrum over not wanting to eat beans and rice again when a squall comes up."

"What's a squall?" I asked.

"It's like that rainstorm we had the other day," Mat explained, "only they usually come with decent gusts of wind, usually from a different direction than what was going on before. So, you know the sails are set according to the direction of the wind, right?" I nodded, Martin having explained it to me one night over cards. "So when the wind shifts dramatically, especially if it's fairly strong, well, sometimes you have to deal with it. In a hurry."

Isaac nodded. "That's why my folks never went offshore with us when we were really little. But we grew up on the boat — Sarah never even knew another home. Kids learn when they need to just shut up and stay out of the way. We did, anyway. I remember a few stormy times on board, when my parents were up in the cockpit in their foulies and Sarah and I were tied into our bunks down below with our lifejackets on. It seems extreme to land people, but it's just what we grew up with. Whatever you get used to is what normal is, right?"

"I guess." That was Martin. He'd been pretty quiet

since we left Costa Rica, and I wondered if it had something to do with what he'd been talking about with Christine or whatever was going on with Tulia. He didn't want to be here and was probably counting the minutes until he could get home. He couldn't be happy about heading off to one of the most remote places in the world — and its commensurately expensive airfares to leave. But he was here, which surprised me a little. I'd imagined that one afternoon he'd go ashore with Isaac and then just never come back. But he turned up every day, even if he looked a little miserable. I wondered why. Maybe he didn't have enough money saved to get home after all.

"People are amazingly adaptable," Isaac went on. "Kids especially. There are plenty of kid boats out there, even in some of the more remote cruising grounds. We all find each other in port, the parents swapping tales and kids being kids. It was a great way to grow up."

"Wasn't it hard to fit in with the group when you were new all the time?" I couldn't imagine how horrible it would be to go to a new place every few months as a kid.

Isaac shook his head. "We were *all* the new kids, that was kind of the point. We didn't know each other, but we all had a common experience to draw on. It's the same for adults — it's so easy to make friends cruising. When you meet another sailor it doesn't matter where you're from or what your backgrounds are, you'll have a whole wealth of stuff in common and things to talk about. I saw it with my parents all the time — they'd meet some new boat, get along with them great, then discover that they were the exact opposite politically or something."

"Doesn't that get awkward?"

"Sometimes, but not as much as it does ashore. Your friendship might change a bit, but we all try to get along. You never know if that guy who loves the stuff you hate will end up being the one helping you pull up a stuck anchor in a gale. That's the one defining thing about the sailing community — it's a real community in that we all do our best to help each other." He shrugged again. "I know I sound like we're all saints, and it's not like that, but I've never found people ashore to be anywhere as genuinely helpful as the average sailor."

"Well, it's kind of self-preservation," Tulia said. "Out here, there's no one else, so we have to help each other. And, like Isaac said, you never know if you're going to be the one who needs help, so it makes sense to at least try to get along."

"Yeah, that's the pragmatist's view," Isaac said. "But I still like to think that this lifestyle makes people a bit less selfish. It's hard to think too much of yourself when you spend so much time being reminded of how small we really are." He stood at the rail and gestured out to sea, the sunset painting the sky in pinks, oranges and yellows. There were no other boats in sight, no sign that there had ever been human beings in existence other than the seven of us. It was humbling and terrifying and at that moment there was nowhere else I'd have wanted to be.

⚓

Darkness crept upon us quickly and the formerly lively crew became instantly sedate. The off-watch crew went down to chill out and try to get some sleep. It was only about seven pm, so I decided to stay up in the cockpit for a while.

The entire feel of the boat seemed to change at night. I had begun to understand some of the readouts on the instruments on the cockpit and could tell that the conditions hadn't really changed. The wind was still in the ten to fifteen knot range, which Martin had explained was a little light for a boat the size of the *Bucket* but was enough to sail by. I was surprised to see Tulia and Isaac take in one of the foresails. When they were done I asked about it.

"We always sail more conservatively at night," Isaac explained. "This isn't a race. It's easier to unfurl a foresail or shake a reef out of the main if the wind dies down than it is to reef later if it builds. This way, even though we're moving more slowly, we've got a buffer built in — in case things pick up later."

"But that's almost half the time," I said. "Does that mean we're sailing less efficiently half the time?"

"Not really," Tulia jumped in. "It's only less efficient if nothing changes and the only rule about the weather is that it will eventually change."

Isaac agreed. "Chances are the wind will pick up as we get into the trades a bit more. Either that or die completely, and either way what we've done now won't be a problem."

I wasn't sure about the logic, but I could see why making things easier for the crew overnight might be worth sacrificing a bit of speed. As I looked out at the now black sky, I could tell that motion of the boat was the same as it had been for hours, but without being able to see the shape of the waves the movement was eerie. The sound of the hull rushing through the water seemed improbably loud and I began to notice other sounds. Creaking and groaning, like the ship was tearing itself apart. I couldn't help but think about how utterly alone we were out here.

I made my way into the main salon, hoping that going inside would make me feel safer. Instead, it amplified the sounds the boat was making. I sunk into a chair then noticed Jimmy across the room, reading a book.

"Um — are these sounds normal?"

His grin was hard to make out in the dim light. "Yeah. Wait until it's a proper breeze — then you'll really hear this boat make some noise."

"It wasn't doing that before," I said, hating the whiny sound of my voice.

"Yeah, it was," he assured me. "You just notice it a lot more at night. There isn't as much other stuff going on, fewer distractions, I think. Don't worry, everything is fine. If it really starts to get to you, just do what I do." He fished an ancient-looking iPod from his pocket. "Crank the tunes."

I was shocked to see him with something so

obviously modern. And *landy*.

He must have seen the expression on my face because he gave a short report of a laugh. "I'm not one of those hippies who thinks you have to just listen to the music of the spheres when you're out here. Shit, woman, I'd never have made it through half my passages if it weren't for midnight disco dance parties all by my lonesome."

I couldn't help but laugh. "It isn't always easy out here, otherwise everyone would do it. So you do what you have to do to get by. For Christine it's yoga, for Mat it's planning. For me it's tunes. You just have to figure out what works for you."

"Thanks." I noticed that while we'd been talking I hadn't heard any of the creaking, but now that I was thinking of it again, it was back. Distraction, that was what Jimmy was talking about. Maybe staying up with the night watch crew wasn't going to be such a great idea for me after all.

Chapter Eight

Shellbacks and Pollywogs

I don't think I slept at all that first night. I'm not sure the boat was rolling any more than it had been when we'd been at anchor at San Juan del Sur, but it felt impossible. I secured my bunk carefully, but every time we lurched even a little bit I felt like I was falling out. I tried jamming myself in with my back against the curtain and my feet pressing against the wall, but then I couldn't relax enough to sleep. When I moved, though, I couldn't help but feel like I was rolling around the bunk like an unsecured pencil on the chart table.

I finally settled into lying on my back in a kind of starfish shape, with my feet braced at the end of my bunk. I've never been any good at sleeping on my back before, and don't think I slept then either, but I rested. Sort of.

Eventually I could see sunlight poking around the edges of the curtain and decided to give up on the charade of sleep. I got dressed in my bunk, not trusting my ability to put on shorts while the boat was moving. How did they do this every day?

I couldn't see anyone down below when I got up, but a couple of the bunks were buttoned up so I tried to be quiet. Not that I could imagine anyone ever getting any sleep under these conditions. I caught a whiff of coffee and nearly cried with relief. I followed my nose up to the cockpit where Mat, Martin and Jimmy were sipping from steaming mugs.

"Coffee?" Martin offered and I nodded silently. I sipped gradually from the lidded mug he handed me and sunk into a seat. Once I was seated, he handed me a tube of sunscreen. I smeared some on then went back to my coffee.

"It takes a while to get used to sleeping under way," Mat said out of nowhere. I guess I looked as rough as I felt. "It gets easier." I just grunted and kept slurping coffee. As the caffeine worked its way through my veins I looked around. There was no sign of land in any direction, no clouds in the sky, not even a seagull.

"There's nothing here," I said.

"The ocean is pretty empty," Martin said with a shrug.

"Whoa." I'd seen maps; I knew that the Pacific has huge landless areas, but I'd expected animals. Birds, fish, the odd pod of dolphins. But there was nothing but sky and sea and us.

"We're making good time," Mat said. "At this rate we'll be having our line-crossing ceremony the same day as landfall."

"We've got a couple of pollywogs to initiate," Jimmy said. I gulped. Initiation? *Pollywogs?*

Mat must have seen the look on my face and laughed. "Don't worry," she said, "this isn't the Navy. Our ritual is all good times, promise."

"Okay." Of all the times to be running on fumes; having some kind of crazy nautical ritual sprung on me the same day as I had to dump the back logs from the—

"Shit." I looked around for somewhere safe to stow my coffee cup, and when I didn't find anything I just handed it to Martin and took off inside.

I practically slid down the ladder to the server room and unlocked the workstation, slipped in and booted the laptop on muscle-memory. I'd totally forgotten to switch the connection over to the satellite and we must have lost cell connection sometime the previous day. I'd only been here a week and already there had been two outages.

Damn it, Devi, you have one job. I opened up the log files and configuration software. My body was going into panic mode: a bit of tunnel vision, heartbeat up, cold sweat, a sense that I had to be doing something all the time. I had about eighteen files up on the small screen and I was trying to read them all while typing the config codes when— I stopped.

The system was up. Packets were coming in and going out in front of my eyes. How was that possible? There was no way were getting a cell signal out, not in the middle of a sea of nothing.

I closed my eyes and took a couple of deep breaths. I opened my eyes and forced myself to focus on one thing at a time. The connection log showed that we'd switched over to the satellite connection just after midnight. I found reference to a script that didn't look familiar, then finally began to use what little brain I still had after my impromptu all-nighter. I had a pretty good idea who had switched the connections.

Manuel.

⚓

Of course one of the first modifications ever made to the system was to automatically switch the network connection. It was obvious now, but I couldn't understand why I hadn't noticed it when I read through the wiki before. I dug into the details and it wasn't elegant but it was efficient. When the signal strength dropped below a certain parameter, the satellite automatically started up. Then a simple but effective network quality test was done to determine which network to use. Easy, peasy.

I did the log cleanup I'd initially meant to do, then packed up. I was securing the workstation when I heard Martin's voice.

"You down there, Devi?"

"Yeah," I shouted back. "Everything okay?"

He came down the ladder. "Oh, sure. I'm just off watch but it's too early to sleep so I wondered if you were busy." He was staring at a point somewhere over my head and I momentarily wondered if there actually was something interesting there. "You're working, though, so never mind."

"I just finished, actually. Can we head up, though? It's not that comfortable down here." He nodded and we went up to the main salon. It was otherwise unoccupied, so I sank into the couch and closed my eyes.

"I can't remember the last time I was this tired."

"Yeah, I don't sleep well the first night or two at sea, either. At least it's not rough."

"Hmph." It did occur to me that the entire time I'd

been down in the server locker, I hadn't once had even a twinge of an upset stomach. Maybe I was too tired to be seasick?

"Hey, Martin?"

"Yeah?"

"Can I ask you something?" He just looked at me, as if to say, *You just did, dummy.* "What are you doing here?"

"Chilling out before trying to get some sleep."

"No, I mean *here* here. On the boat." I knew I shouldn't be asking him this. It was totally none of my business, but I was too tired to stop myself. "Look, I'm sorry. I didn't mean to eavesdrop but I overheard you talking to Christine the other day. About going home? Every time you went ashore I kept expecting you to not come back. But here you are. How come?"

He smiled at me and shook his head. "I wouldn't have left without saying good-bye. What kind of a guy do you think I am? Anyway, I have a contract. I agreed to work on the Bucket until the end of April, and I'm not going to break my contract even though it means it'll be harder to get home. I'm pretty sure that the extra pay will make up for the difference in the flights. Besides, how else am I ever going to get to see the Galápagos?"

I chuckled. "Yeah, there's that. I didn't even know that people could go there. Isn't it some kind of natural wildlife refuge?"

"Kind of but not really," Martin said. "Isaac's been there before, and he said that people live there. Like full time. It's not the remote nature wonderland everyone thinks it is."

"Weird."

"I know, right?"

That reminded me. "So what's up with this line-crossing thing? Is this the equator deal?" He nodded. "Do I need to be worried?"

"I dunno. I've never crossed the equator before either. I think we just dress up and drink champagne. That's what happens on cruise ships."

"How do you know what happens on cruise ships?"

"My folks went on one for their anniversary a few years before they died."

I felt my face freeze. "Oh," I stammered. "Uh, sorry—"

"Really, you don't have to say anything every time I talk about my parents. I miss them and I wish they were still around, but I'm okay, you know? It would be nice to be able to talk about them without everyone getting all maudlin."

"Sorry," I repeated, cringing at myself as I realized what I'd said, but Martin just laughed.

"You really are tired," he said and I nodded. "I'm going to grab a sandwich, then try to get a few zees. You should probably do the same."

"Yeah," I said, but I still didn't believe it was possible to sleep with the boat moving. Though as I stood up and started walking toward the galley, it occurred to me that I hadn't really noticed the motion while we were talking.

⚓

I don't know what time it was when I crawled into my bunk, but Jimmy hadn't even started on supper and the sun was high in the sky. The curtain blocked out most of the light though, and the peanut butter sandwich I'd eaten kept my stomach from growling. The thought of trying to read was beyond impossible and I didn't have any movies on my phone. That was bad planning, I thought as I squirmed in my bunk, trying to get comfortable. I needed to rest and a dumb movie would have been perfect. I lay there, trying to remember the plot of the last superhero movie I watched when somehow I slipped into the fog of sleep.

When I woke it was dark, both in the confines of my bunk and when I peeked past the curtain. I could sure feel the boat moving now, but it didn't feel bad. I popped out my earplugs and was assaulted by noise. Creaking, groaning and wind.

I picked my way up to the cockpit, donning my PFD as I reached the door. I stuck my head out and said, "What's going on?"

She must not have heard me open the door, because Christine shrieked at the sound of my voice.

"Jeez, Devi, what are you doing up? It's like three in the morning."

Whoa. I must have slept for ten hours or more. "Sorry. My rhythm's all out of whack." I moved over to a nearby seat and looked around. It felt like we were moving really fast, but now that she'd recovered from my unexpected appearance, Christine didn't seem concerned. And she was the only one in the cockpit. "Everything okay?"

"Oh, yeah," she said. "The wind picked up a bit a few hours ago, which is great. We're making ten knots." She grinned and I guessed that was fast. "I hate it when we're doing anything less than six. I know Mat prefers to sail even if it's slow, and the tree-hugger in me is fine with that, but I can't help it; it drives me crazy. This is way better."

"So ten knots — what's that in land terms?"

"A bit more than ten miles an hour."

It was a good thing I wasn't drinking anything, because I'd have spit it all over myself. "Ten miles an hour? Like—" I did some math in my head, "twice as fast as a person can run?"

She frowned. "I dunno. I guess?"

"Ten miles per hour is like a granny on a bicycle."

She laughed. "Boats are slow. Remember *S Cargo*? That's the whole point of their name — they're slow."

"I had no idea." I looked over the side and watched the water rushing past. It was sure it was a whole lot faster than ten miles per hour, but I looked at the instruments and saw the boat speed indicator reading 10.2. "No wonder air travel changed the world."

"True enough," she said, "but look at it this way — at this rate, we'll make landfall tomorrow."

⚓

That afternoon Mat caught a tuna, which was the absolute highlight of the day. Boats are slow, the ocean is mostly empty, and days at sea are mostly long stretches of nothing happening. I heard Tulia saying that on most passages catching a fish was the most exciting thing that happened, which was the way she liked it.

I always assumed fishing was fairly straightforward, but it took a long time to tire out the fish once it got the lure and getting it aboard was a real process. I had no idea tuna were so huge! I'd only ever had tuna from a can. Obviously, the crew knew what they were doing, but when blood started spurting all over the aft deck I decided that I urgently had to go down below to check the servers.

If catching the fish was a challenge, it was worth it. The tuna tasted great and Jimmy cooked it to perfection. He also made ceviche with the last tomatoes and some fresh cilantro he tended in a small herb garden in the galley. I'd never had it before, but it was all delicious. We ate with gusto, but when we couldn't eat any more there was still loads left. "No one's going to starve on this ship," Jimmy said as we leaned back from the table, bellies full.

I helped Martin clear the dishes. I was careful to take only what I could easily carry in one hand, but the boisterous motion of the boat combined with my fatigued mind and body. I'd just turned the corner to the ladder down toward the galley when I completely lost my balance. I didn't fall down the companionway at least, but I did drop four bowls and assorted cutlery all over the place.

"Shit," I heard Martin shout from down below.

"Sorry," I called back. "You okay?"

"Yeah. But it's raining forks down here!"

I got down on my hands and knees to collect the stuff that had stayed up on deck level. There was a slight sheen of tomato juice and fish all over everything. I corralled the cutlery and bowls, then very carefully went down the ladder. I handed the stuff to Martin who grinned at me, then I caught a wet washcloth in the face.

"Better go swab the deck before anyone else goes ass over teakettle." Jimmy smirked at me and I dejectedly went back up to clean the floor.

When I'd finished cleaning and the adrenaline had worn off, I found that I could barely keep my eyes open. "I don't know how I'm going to get back to normal after this," I said, after I'd yawned for about the eighth time.

Martin shrugged. "We're all screwed up after a passage, but usually a good night's sleep in port does the job. Passages are tiring, even when you can sleep, so the first night at anchor is kind of like magic. The boat's still, everything is quiet, and you've got that sense of accomplishment to boot. I always sleep like a log."

"Well, I could use some log time. Like, right now." I climbed the ladder and headed for my bunk.

I was the only one in the bunk room, but there could probably have been a party going on in there and I'd have never known. I had enough time to recognize that the motion of the boat was rocking me to sleep, when I conked out.

🜄

At least the sun was up when I woke the next day. It was still early, though — the night and day watches were handing over when I poked my head out to the cockpit.

"Hey, good to see you up," Isaac said. "We'll be crossing the equator soon and you'll be needed for a very important job." He grinned and waggled his eyebrows at me.

I'd forgotten all about that mysterious ritual. I looked around, trying to gauge the situation, but it looked like any other morning at sea. Mat was poring over the chart plotter, Tulia coiled lines and squinted up at the sails, Christine marked her place in her book and went down for a nap. No one seemed to be the least bit concerned. Only Isaac was behaving oddly, and he disappeared down below.

"I think we'll be making landfall tonight," Mat told us. "Probably after dark, which isn't ideal, but it should be before midnight. We made good time."

"What happens then?" I asked.

She shrugged. "I'll go ashore and stand in a queue all day, if things haven't changed since the last time I was here." She rolled her eyes but I didn't think she was as annoyed as her words implied. "The company springs for park passes for all of us, so once I've checked in and gotten those, you all can go ashore. The anchorage at Baquerizo Moreno isn't great, so I'll want to move on to Isla Isabela in a day or two. There are some decent restaurants in town and there should still be time to get in on a snorkelling tour or something, though. It's worth doing, trust me."

Snorkeling tour? Restaurants? *Town?* Was this really the Galápagos? I was about to ask more about what to expect when Mat burst into laughter. I turned to see what had struck her fancy and was greeted by Isaac. Or at least, I was pretty sure it was Isaac.

He was shirtless, wearing a mop head as a wig, a paper crown perched precariously on top. He carried a bottle of champagne in one hand and in the other brandished one of Jimmy's barbecue forks with a bunch of seashells stuck to it with tape.

"I am King Neptune," he bellowed. "Here to induct these pollywogs into the fraternity of my children."

"Who's got a camera?" Tulia shouted.

"Go find one and get the rest of the crew," Mat said, still laughing. "You're outdoing yourself, mate."

Isaac ignored her completely and nestled the bottle in a canvas pocket full of rope. The others began to come up to the cockpit, Christine glowering and ready to take a strip off of someone.

"I was just falling aslee—" She caught a look at Isaac and her face froze. Then she started to laugh. "Okay, this is worth missing a little sleep."

"What's going on?" Martin said, taking in the full cockpit. "Have we arrived?"

"Not yet," Mat said. "We're having a visit from the local authorities."

Martin's face took on a concerned expression until he caught a glimpse of Isaac. "What the—?"

"Honourable shellbacks!" Isaac looked toward Mat and Tulia, then gestured for Christine to join them. She giggled as she wedged herself into a seat by the other women. "It is time to induct these pollywogs into the sacred order of the Children of Neptune." Martin and I shared a glance. "Where's my deputy?"

Jimmy came out on deck with a tray of snacks — heavy on the fish — and a sheaf of papers. "My liege," he said, handing Isaac the papers, and winking at me and Martin. Then he put down the food and went over to where the others were waiting.

Isaac glanced at the GPS readout, paused for a moment, then began to intone. "It is a time-honoured tradition among mariners to commemorate those who have crossed the equator by sea. While it is ultimately an arbitrary point in the journey, it symbolizes a personal milestone. There is more to becoming a shellback than the numbers on a screen — you both boarded this vessel as landlubbers, but now you are sailors." He handed us both fancy-looking papers with our names in hand-written calligraphic script proclaiming that the bearers were now honourable shellbacks as of this date, signed Isaac Sloane, per Neptune Rex. I tried to keep my expression solemn, but it was hard not to laugh.

"Congratulations," Mat said, popping the cork on the bottle of champagne. She filled glasses and handed them to us. Martin went to take a sip, but Jimmy stopped him.

"Hang on, lad. First drop's for merciful Poseidon." Martin frowned, but waited until everyone had a glass. Then Isaac went over to the side and poured a bit overboard.

"We ask King Neptune for fair winds and following seas."

"And if we can't have that," Mat said, "we'll take a quick passage."

Tulia laughed at that and dumped half her glass overboard. "Hear, hear."

The rest of us followed suit, more of the bubbly ending up in the drink than in us. That wasn't so bad, considering that it was still morning and the thought of drinking a lot of alcohol didn't seem terribly appealing at sea.

Now that the official ceremony was over, Isaac went down to change and Christine went back to bed. The rest of us hung out in the cockpit, nibbling on Jimmy's snacks and chatting. There was an excitement among us, though we all were careful not to talk about specifics. It was as if there were some kind of superstition that if we talked about when we would arrive that we would jinx it somehow.

I'd settled into my usual spot in the cockpit — out of the way — and was deep into reading when Martin squealed.

"Are you okay?" I dropped my book and went over to where he was standing, ready to grab the first aid kit.

"Land," he said, breathless. "I think I can see land!"

"That's not land," I said, "is it? It looks like a cloud to me."

"Maybe," Martin said, sounding a bit deflated. "I really thought it was—"

We stared at whatever it was, debating the possibilities for several minutes before Martin remembered the chart plotter.

The boat was represented by a small triangle in the middle of the screen, its course a dotted line heading off to the bottom left of the picture. Where there was, indeed, an island!

"Yes! Martin, you were right, that *is* land!"

"All right!" He raised his arms in the field-goal gesture, then I found myself enveloped in a hug. I was startled but before I could say anything he'd let go and bounded off down below.

"Hey, you guys," he shouted. "Land ho!"

⚓

The hours between when Martin first spied land and we arrived were slower than anything I'd ever before experienced. It had only been a few days since we'd left, but hadn't realized how much I'd been anticipating arrival — it was like a birthday, graduation and Halloween all rolled into one. It didn't help that the routine markers of time I'd grown accustomed to on the passage — naps for the night watch crew, the early evening meal together, regular watch changes — were all suspended. Everyone was awake, most of us openly gawping at the rugged landscape as it painstakingly came more clearly into view.

While it seemed to take forever to make landfall, it wasn't boring. We'd been more or less following a straight line since we'd left Costa Rica — the rhumb line, Isaac called it. It meant that there wasn't a lot of sail work or steering, just the odd adjustment for a shift in the wind. Now we were actually trying to get somewhere that we could see, and I figured out from the chart that our anchorage was actually on the other side of that island. Mat and Isaac were both busy plotting the course and the others all took turns on the lines.

In between sail chores, we marvelled at the dramatic increase in the amount of wildlife. There had been so little to see on most of the passage, but as we neared the island of San Cristóbal, birds began to darken the sky. I was watching them with Christine when a pair of unfamiliar-looking birds came close to the boat.

"Show us your feet," she yelled.

"What?"

"I want to see if they are blue-footed boobies," she explained, peering up at the fat brown birds. "I've seen the yellow-footed ones before, but the blue ones only live here."

I squinted, trying to get a better look at their feet, but they were tucked up under their bellies. We never did find out which ones they were. Later, a shout of "dolphins!" came from the foredeck. I carefully picked my way forward to see literally hundreds of dolphins coming toward the boat. This was what I'd imagined sailing to be like, but I hadn't been prepared for the reality. From a distance it looked almost like the water was boiling, and as they neared I could hear the sound of them splashing. It was incredible.

I discovered that I was shaking as a couple of them came right up to the front of the boat, swimming under the bow and playing in the wake. One of them turned on its side and looked right at me, blowing out its blowhole. Christine stood next to me, clapping her hands and hooting. Martin had his phone out, taking what I imagined would be Loch Ness Monster-quality video. The pod stayed for about half an hour, then as abruptly as they'd arrived they appeared to tire of us and took off in search of something more interesting.

I sank down to the deck and just sat there, stunned.

"That never gets old." I hadn't even noticed that Isaac was up there with us. He grinned at me and I found that I'd still lost my voice. "I've been sailing my whole life, probably seen a million porpoises and dolphins, and it still makes my day. Never forget how lucky you are to be able to experience this." He left me to my thoughts and the spray of our bow wake.

⚓

Darkness fell even more quickly here than it had in Costa Rica, since we were so close to the equator. We began to round the island around dusk and while sailing into the sunset was beautiful I found it impossible to see anything in front of us. The orange-yellow glow reflected on the ocean's surface seemed to obscure everything. Soon it was completely dark and I could see the lights of town ahead. The captain had been right; after nearly a week at sea it looked like a whole city. I was mesmerized by the lights and never did understand how the crew managed to drop the anchor in among the other boats in the bay. They did it, though, and we were parked before midnight.

Being at anchor isn't completely stable, but after being under way it felt solid as a rock to me. That night, I slept like the dead, but woke early the next day. I didn't know what to expect, but I didn't want to miss out on anything. I'd never been one of those kids who lives at the zoo or goes crazy over animals, but this was the opportunity of a lifetime.

I found Jimmy and Tulia in the galley and gratefully accepted a cup of coffee. "Mat's gone ashore already," Tulia said. "The rest of us are stuck on board until we're cleared in. Supposedly the officials can be real hard-asses here."

Jimmy shrugged. "It's better than it used to be in South America. Sure, it takes time, but at least you know what you'll have to pay and who you have to pay it to. None of this 'my brother the laundry inspector needs another twenty bucks' business."

Tulia smiled at him indulgently then asked me if I was hungry. I nodded, scared to say anything in case it broke the truce we seemed to be enjoying. We scrounged up some breakfast then went up above decks where we found the rest of the crew. I was astounded. The bay was chock full of boats, mostly modern looking sailboats, flying flags from all over the world. We were anchored near a cliff at the mouth of the bay, but ashore I should see several buildings, a small dock and even what looked like an outdoor restaurant.

"Wow. This is *not* what I expected."

"Me neither," Tulia said. "But when you think about it it's not that crazy. Lots of tourists come through here, plus there's all the scientists who are stationed here or visiting. They need hotels and restaurants and grocery stores, right?"

"I guess."

Waiting for Mat to get back so we could go ashore was maddening, but there was plenty to do on board to get things squared away after several days at sea. Everyone was busy tidying lines and washing the salt off of everything, so I kept out of their way by checking on the system. There was cell service here, so I switched the network over and did a quick speed test. It was pretty slow for cell, but better than satellite, so I left it. I turned on my phone to discover a weak open wifi network, then spent a frustrating half hour almost getting my email. I eventually gave up, hoping the connection would be better ashore. Assuming we were ever allowed ashore.

Mat returned after four o'clock in the afternoon. I took one look at her face and knew not to say a word.

"We're clear." She didn't say anything else, just handed us each a packet of papers. I opened mine to find my passport, duly stamped by the Ecuadorean officials, a tourist permit and a credit card-sized parks pass. The part of the documentation that was most clear said I could be in the Galápagos for 28 days, but the rest was a bunch of rules about where I could go on my own and where I needed an accredited guide. It all seemed unnecessarily complicated.

"Do you get all this?" I asked Jimmy who'd quickly flipped through his papers then jammed them in a pocket.

He nodded. "Money grab, mostly. But we're cool to go ashore now. You have to take a water taxi, but it's cheap and it means you're not stuck waiting for Isaac. Don't worry about the stuff in the papers — it just means we can't go anchor anywhere. If you don't go AWOL you'll be fine."

I snorted. I wasn't likely to wander off on my own, here or anywhere. There was more than enough adventure to be had sticking with the group. "Hang on," I said. "I don't have any local currency."

"You sure?" Jimmy asked. "They use US dollars."

"Seriously? I might have some."

He dug around in his pockets then handed me a few quarters. "Just in case." I grinned and thanked him, then went down below to my bunk to see if I had any American money.

I was stuffing a five into my wallet when Isaac shouted, "Taxi's here!"

"Shit!" Christine flew past me en route to her bunk. "Wait for me!"

I grabbed my bag, jammed my sandals on my feet and climbed up to the deck where I ran into Martin. "It's going to be a full boat," he said. I nodded as we waited our turn to load into the water taxi. Christine just made it, then the pilot revved the engine and we wove our way through the anchored boats to the dock.

"What the—?" I thought I was prepared for anything, but I had to fight the urge to rub my eyes in disbelief.

"Are those seals?" Martin articulated the question on my mind.

"Sea lions, actually," Tulia said. "They sure don't seem to mind all the people." It was obvious that they weren't afraid of us at all. There were dozens of them all over the dock and as I looked further ashore, they were all over the sidewalks as well. One was lounging on a park bench. A pair of them half-heartedly chased a guy with an ice-cream cone. It seemed to me that they were just going through the motions — they looked like they could have easily caught him if they'd really wanted to.

As we pulled up to the dock I found myself getting a bit nervous. These guys were not small. We have seals and sea lions back home and I'd seen them snoring on the rocks at the shore many times. But I'd never been this close and never seen so many. I certainly hadn't had to run a gauntlet of them just to get to the sidewalk before.

There were a few people on the taxi when we'd boarded, so we all followed their lead and stepped nonchalantly on to the dock — well, as nonchalantly as possible given that we were getting the stink-eye from a pack of creatures that probably weighed a ton apiece. They were cool, though. One of them snorted at Martin as he walked past, but that was the extent of their concern for us.

We got to a cartoony map of the island posted on a pillar in the square by the dock. "There isn't really enough time left in the day to go too far," Isaac said. "But take a look at what you might like to do. Mat said we'll have a free day ashore tomorrow, so make the most of it. I don't know how much time we'll have here." He pointed at a couple of the tour operators listed on the guide. "These guys are good, and I've always gotten a last minute spot on a tour. Or you can just hire a taxi to take you to a couple of the snorkelling spots or the tortoise sanctuary. If a bunch of you want to all chip in that can be the cheapest way to see stuff."

He turned and pointed down the shoreline. "I'm going over to that cafe to see if I can get a burger. If I don't see you there, meet you back at the *Bucket*. Don't stay out too late." He winked at us and wandered off towards the restaurants.

I peered at the map. There was a seemingly endless list of tour companies offering a bewildering array of packages. "I can't decide what to do," Tulia said. "Any of you guys want to try the taxi thing?"

"I'm in," I said, glad that someone else had taken the lead. Martin agreed. Jimmy said he'd already made plans and Christine had an organized tour in mind.

"Three should be enough to make it reasonable," Jimmy said. "I think it's like fifty bucks for the day."

"Damn it!" I said. "I've only got a five."

"There's a bank machine over there." Tulia jerked her thumb at a small set of shops.

"I don't know why I'm still surprised to see things like bank machines everywhere," I said. "And honestly, I kind of forgot all about money since I've been on board."

"I know what you mean," Martin said. "It's nice not to think about it for once."

I took out some cash then waited for the others to do the same. "So what do you think?" Jimmy said after we were done with the bank. "Beer o'clock?"

⚓

There wasn't much to separate the restaurants along the waterfront — they all offered the same items at more or less the same prices. So we chose one with an outdoor table that seated us all and wasn't entirely overrun by sea lions. The others all ordered the local beer and I felt like a celebration of some sort was in order, too, so I asked for a glass of white wine. It wasn't great but it wasn't bad either and we enjoyed our drinks with a few nibbles Jimmy picked off the menu.

"You've been here before," Tulia said to Jimmy. "What should we do tomorrow?"

"Well," he put down his beer and looked out to sea thoughtfully. "When we get to Isabela there's plenty of swimming and snorkelling right in the anchorage, so I wouldn't pay for that unless it's exceptional." He turned to Christine. "You're doing an all-day boat trip, right?" She nodded. "Yeah, that would be worthwhile. A short one, though, I wouldn't bother. So, if you're just getting a taxi to take you around, I'd go to the tortoise sanctuary and maybe ask the driver for a good free swimming hole. They know their way around and you'll probably find something good and save a few dollars."

It seemed like a haphazard way to spend what might be our only day here, but I couldn't afford a hundred dollar organized tour, so it was probably my best bet. And a tortoise sanctuary sounded pretty cool. We ordered a few more rounds at the bar, but when the sun started going down I passed on a refill.

"I think I'm still running on fumes from being at sea; I'm going to grab a water taxi and get an early night."

"Me, too," Christine said, standing. "I've got a full day tomorrow." Jimmy picked up his beer and eyed it. Then he looked at Martin and Tulia, downed his beer and stood.

"Yeah, I'm too old for this anyway. You two have a good time." He nudged me and Christine and we left Martin and Tulia looking a bit confused.

"What was that all about?" Christine asked when we were on the water taxi.

"Those two could use a bit of time on their own, eh?"

"What do you mean?" I said. "There isn't anything going on between them."

"I know," Jimmy said. "That's the problem."

⚓

"Is he always like that?" Christine and I were alone in the main salon, each of us in our pajamas with our books, but gossiping instead.

"He's never tried to play matchmaker before," she said, "not that I know of anyway. But we've never had two crew members with such obvious interest in each other."

"Really?" That kind of explained the way Tulia acted around me, since Martin spent more time with me than her. Of course, there wasn't ever going to be anything between us, but she didn't know that, I guess.

Christine shrugged. "Yeah. They used to hang out all the time, but then he started talking about leaving and things got weird and they kind stopped hanging out. That's around when you got here. But there's something up with them for sure. We all noticed it — well, all of us except them, I guess."

"Huh." I could see why neither of them was trying to pursue a relationship; after all Martin wasn't going to be on the boat much longer. It was probably a matter of days at this point. What was Jimmy thinking? If they did get together now it would just mean they'd have to say good-bye. The thought reminded me of Jeannette and I felt my throat tighten up. I realized I hadn't thought of her at all since we left Costa Rica, and that somehow made me feel worse.

"I'm going to turn in." I made it out of the common room before the tears came. Damn it, I hated crying. I hid in the head until I was done then lay awake feeling sorry for myself until I heard Martin and Tulia come back. I couldn't tell how their night on the town had gone and I didn't want to know. The thought of anyone finding romance, even if only for a few days, just made me feel worse.

It took a long time to get to sleep.

Everyone was up with the sun the next day, except Christine, who'd left so early that I didn't even see her. Tulia, Martin, and I packed bags with snorkelling gear, towels, water bottles and a sack of sandwiches Jimmy made us, then we stood on the side deck watching for a water taxi. I wondered what it would be like with the three of us alone together — I hoped I wasn't going to become the stereotypical third wheel.

The water taxis reminded me a bit of the pangas in Central America, only more tricked out. The hulls were the same canoe-shaped open fibreglass, but there were padded seats along the sides and a roof overhead. It kind of reminded me of the harbour taxis in Vancouver, only way bigger and more industrial. Tulia flagged one down and as it made its way toward us we headed aft to the swim step.

Which had been colonized by a pair of sea lions. The stink was amazing. "Shoo!" Tulia shouted at them, waving her hands. One of them grunted at us, snorting obscene fish breath in our faces. It reared up, but didn't vacate the premises. The other one seemed to still be sleeping.

"Hey," I said, feeling pretty silly to be talking to a sea lion, "get off! Come on, get!" More snorting but this time they both responded. The water taxi pulled up then, and the driver leaned over and yelled something at them in Spanish. He brandished a broom, but didn't come close to touching them. That did the trick and with a chorus of grunts and much flapping of flippers, they reluctantly slid off the boat and into the water. *Ort ort!*

The swim step was gross, but at least it was passable. I felt bad about just leaving it, but we had to go. Still, I felt sorry for whoever ended up dealing with it. I made a mental note to do something nice for whoever it was.

On our way ashore I noticed that the *Bucket* wasn't alone in being turned into a sea lion hangout. It seemed like every boat that had any area that was accessible to them was covered in sea lions. A few people had tried to dissuade them by tying lines across their transoms or covering their steps with random stuff — fenders, cushions, a kayak — but even that hadn't always worked.

"Wow," Martin said. "They really own the place, don't they?"

"Well, they were here first," Tulia said. "I'm just amazed at how comfortable they are around people. I mean, obviously no one is hunting them around here, but you'd still think they'd be a bit more — I don't know, *wild*."

"Isn't that a thing in places were species have developed without natural predators, though?" I said. "They just don't have any fear. That's why so many of these unique species are endangered."

"Or already extinct," Martin said. "That's the story of the dodo, right?"

We were spared more of this depressing discussion by our arrival at the dock. Tulia asked the skipper, "¿Dónde está los taxis?" and after a bit of gesturing and repeating things, we were herded off down the street. Several small trucks were lined up, their drivers unobtrusively shilling for fares. Martin and I let Tulia do all the talking; her Spanish wasn't great but at least she could communicate. She negotiated a deal for the day with stops at a couple of free swimming spots and a trip out to the Interpretation Centre.

I balked when the driver clearly indicated that we should all just pile into the bed of the truck. "Seriously?"

Tulia shrugged. "It's an adventure." She chucked her bag then climbed in after it. Martin followed suit and I guessed it was just what was done, so I did, too. There wasn't much traffic and we weren't driving very fast, but it still felt unnecessarily dangerous. It was nice to be outside, though, and we got a great view of the coastline as we drove out to a small beach. It only took about five minutes and we clambered out to find the place deserted. I wondered if we were being scammed.

I'd worn my swimsuit under my shorts and tank top, and stuck my clothes into my bag hoping to keep the sand and salt water off them. I donned flippers and a snorkel like a pro — or at least, like I'd done it before — and waddled over to the shore. I waded in and began to swim around.

At first there wasn't much to see and I was convinced that the taxi driver had just stolen our stuff and taken off. I popped out of the water to see our bags where we'd left them and the taxi driver over by the truck talking on his cell phone. There was a splash behind me and then I heard Martin's voice. "Check this out!"

I swam over to where he was to see a giant turtle swimming underneath us. "Omigod!" I said into my snorkel, which sounded even to my ears like Charlie Brown's teacher, but I couldn't help myself. It was enormous, maybe the size of a kid's red wagon. Like the sea lions, it didn't seem to care about us at all, just kept swimming lazily around. Tulia dove down, bubbles coming out of her snorkel, and ran her hand over its shell. The water was warm enough, but I got goosebumps when I saw that. I didn't have the nerve to do it myself — diving? touching a wild animal? — but just watching it was incredible. At that moment, I wouldn't have cared if the taxi driver did steal our clothes. Which, of course, he didn't.

⚓

The drive up to the Interpretive Centre wasn't that interesting, but we were all still on a high from our swim. We babbled among ourselves about what we'd seen, even though we could barely hear over the trucks' engine. When we got to the centre, Tulia and the driver talked for a bit, then she told us that he was going to leave us there for a couple of hours and would pick us up later.

I read the panels on the walls of the small room inside the building, explaining the history of the Galápagos tortoises and the background of the centre.

"Come on," Tulia said, pulling at my sleeve. "You can read about this stuff anytime; let's go see them!" She seemed to have gotten over whatever it was that bugged her about me.

We walked along the neatly groomed paths into an area that had been kept more or less natural. It was like going for a hike in a national park — which, when I really thought about it, is pretty much what it was. We weren't moving very fast, keeping our eyes open for something interesting when Martin stopped. He pointed wordlessly and there it was. A giant tortoise, probably five times as massive as the turtle we'd swum with. It was eating some leaves, its tail poking out of the back of its shell and its giant feet ambling along in the dirt. Tulia made a small, excited noise.

"There are two of them," I whispered, spying another tortoise half-hidden further in the foliage. We stood there watching them for a while, then reluctantly left them to their inscrutable business. We saw several more tortoises along the paths, which ended at the nursery.

"No one's making tortoise soup anymore," Tulia said. "How come they need protecting?"

"If you'd read the stuff back there," I said, grinning to take the sting out, "you'd know that it's because of the other animals people brought to the islands. Cats, dogs, goats — they eat the eggs or just break them."

"Jeez," Tulia said, making a face. "Poor little guys."

"They are seriously adorable," Martin said, his face

close to the chicken wire that covered the large pens where the tiny tortoises were kept. "Look at their little mouths!"

Until then I wouldn't have thought that watching something eat could be so entertaining, but Martin was right. Watching their tiny beaks tear at the bamboo shoots was mesmerizing.

"It's a good thing they're locked up; I don't think I'd be able to stop myself from stealing one if they were just running around loose."

Tulia laughed at Martin. "I don't think these guys ever run anywhere. And what would you do, stick one in your pocket? Hey, sailor, is that a tortoise down there or are you just happy to see me?" Martin's face turned red and he ignored her laughter.

We could easily have stayed longer, but our taxi truck returned and we continued on our way. We stopped at a couple of other beaches and visited a freshwater lake in a crater. It was nice to wash the salt off in the lake and lie in the sun, but soon it was time to go.

As we were leaving I turned to Martin and Tulia. "That has to be the best twenty bucks I've ever spent."

⚓

When we got back to the boat, Mat announced that we'd be leaving for Isla Isabela the next morning bright and early. I was dead tired, so stayed aboard along with most of the crew and had an early night. Even so, we were underway when I woke up.

It felt strangely normal to be at sea again, even if we

seemed to be much closer to the islands than was prudent. I found myself glancing at the chart plotter constantly to reassure myself that we weren't going to hit anything. "I never would have thought that I'd be nervous about being close to shore," I said to Isaac as we passed a rocky point.

"It's not the sea that's dangerous," he answered, "it's the sharp stuff at the edges you have to worry about."

I left the navigating to the pros and went down to check on my servers. It hadn't taken long to develop that parental sense of ownership — at least I hadn't given them cutesy nicknames. Yet. The system had automatically switched over to the satellite and I watched someone's data transfer at what a few weeks ago I would have thought of as an unacceptably slow pace. Now, I just made a note in log that all was working within parameters and put everything away. It's amazing how we adapt to different circumstances, how quickly something that was utterly foreign can become the new normal.

⚓

Isla Isabela was what I'd imagined the Galápagos would be. At least, more so than San Cristóbal. There was still a town and restaurants and bakeries and cars, but the anchorage was ringed by a reef which was home to Christine's promised blue-footed boobies as well as Galápagos penguins. Penguins! They swam around the anchored boats as if it were the most natural thing in the world. Which, I guess, it was.

Once we got anchored, Mat and Isaac went ashore

to deal with the officials and the rest of us stood on the side deck gawking at the sights in the anchorage. A school of small fish darted like silver lightning though the clear water, followed by penguins and sea lions. "Shark!" Christine shouted from the port side, so all of us on the other side of the boat shot over to see. At first there wasn't anything there, then I saw the tell-tale fin poking up. It wasn't large, maybe about a metre long, but it was a shark all right. It joined the other larger animals in chasing after the fish ball, and we watched the show until they all moved too far away to see.

Later, Isaac returned with the dinghy and we all loaded in. There was a small bar right on the dinghy dock, which also served as one edge of a small swimming lagoon. A bunch of kids were snorkelling around the lagoon when we arrived. "We'll get the kayaks out tomorrow," Isaac said. "It's great to paddle around by the reef — bring your camera."

We sat at the bar, coming up with plans to fill the next few days. Mat arrived a few rounds in and we had a crew meeting.

"It all depends on the weather, but we'll probably stay here two or three days. There's some work to do to get the boat ready for the crossing, but there will be lots of time for sightseeing and fun, I promise." She grinned and popped open another beer.

"Crossing?" I asked.

Isaac nodded. "After this, our next stop is French Polynesia. We're crossing the Pacific."

Already? I'd known that was the plan, of course, but somehow I'd assumed it would be later. Much later. Like when I was ready for it.

The bar party broke up and Martin and I walked over to the dinghy dock. We sat on the edge, our feet dangling in the lagoon.

"It's not like I'm not having a great time — I am," I said, kicking water absent-mindedly. "I don't even really miss home. But this is the real deal. What if we hit a container? What if there's a storm? What if we get hit by lightning?"

"What if you were home and got hit by a car?" Martin said. "That's way more likely. Look around you, Devi. Most people never get to see this." He pointed at a nearby bench. "That's an iguana sitting there, for Pete's sake. When does that ever happen at home?"

I knew he was right, but I wasn't done freaking out. "Since when are you Mister Adventure? You're going home, anyway. How come it's okay for you to want to go back to a normal life but I can't?"

"I—" He pulled his feet out of the water and hugged his knees. "I don't know. It's different."

"How is it different? What do you have waiting for you back home that I don't? A girlfriend who isn't your girlfriend anymore? Yeah, me too, and that's not exactly something pulling me back. A blisteringly awesome career? Nope. So why not stay on board?"

I'd probably gone too far, but I didn't care. I was scared but he was right, this was probably going to be the single coolest thing I'd ever do in my life. And the rest of the crew were fine, especially now that Tulia wasn't shooting me daggers, but Martin was the one who made me feel like everything was going to be okay. I knew I was being selfish, but I didn't want him to go.

"I don't see you signing up for a full time gig," he said, staring out at the lagoon. "It's easy for you when you know you'll be back home in a few months no matter what. You don't know what it's like, Devi."

He was right, I didn't. "I'm sorry. It's none of my business. I just..." I stood up and looked down at him. "I'm just going to miss you, that's all."

I put my sandals on and went to find a ride back to the *Bucket*.

⚓

Martin avoided me for a while after that conversation. I can't say I blamed him — who wants a needy friend right when you're finally getting out of a job you didn't really want in the first place? I took one of the kayaks around the bay. It was nice to spend a little time on my own. I hadn't noticed how close the quarters were on the boat until I was paddling around by myself. I took the kayak in close to the reef at the head of the bay and marvelled at how close the penguins on the rocks let me get. I understood why Isaac had suggested a camera, but I wasn't willing to risk bringing my phone in this tippy boat. I was already soaked through.

I hung around with the penguins, watching them waddle around on the rocks like ungainly toddlers, then gracefully dive into the water. They were obviously in their element as they swam; it was uncanny how much they looked like they were flying. I didn't know how much time had passed when I heard what sounded like a series of small detonations from out in the bay. I clumsily maneuvered the kayak around and felt my jaw literally drop as I saw hundreds of birds make a funnel shape in the air as they dove beak-first into the water. The sound of them pouring into the lagoon was what I'd heard.

"This is unbelievable," I said aloud, though there was no one but the penguins to hear me. The diving flock was between me and the *Byte Bucket* and there was no way I was going to put myself between all those sharp, hungry beaks and their dinner, so I stayed put until they'd caught all the fish they wanted.

Once they'd moved on, I paddled back, the grinning shark face painted on the *Bucket*'s hull an easy target. I was wrestling the kayak on deck when two arms reached down to help. "Hey," Tulia said as she helped me get the boat up. "What's going on with you and Martin?"

"Nothing's going on! I'm not—" I stopped myself from talking and pulled the kayak away from Tulia. I tried and failed to shove it onto its mounting bracket.

"I thought... well, you know." Her face darkened and she wasn't looking at me. "But he told me about your ex, and — you don't like guys, right?"

"Well, I'm gay, if that's what you mean." Oh, could we *please* not be having this conversation? "Anyway," I deflected, "what's going on between the two of *you*?"

I knew I was being an asshole, but I couldn't help it. She didn't get mad, though, just looked sad and sighed. "I don't know," she said. "We kind of hooked up but then it got weird. He isn't talking to me and now he isn't talking to you. I know he wants to go home, and I told him he shouldn't stay because of me, but that doesn't mean..."

"It doesn't mean you won't miss him." I finished. She looked at me and I shrugged. "I like him, too. Not like you do, but I really wish he were sticking around. He isn't talking to me because I yelled at him and told him not to go." It sounded so childish saying it out loud. Tulia just nodded.

"I'm scared he's going to leave without saying good-bye."

"I'm not that much of a jerk." We both jumped at the sound of Martin's voice. I didn't know how long he'd been there, but it was obviously long enough. "Besides, the other day I heard someone say something really smart — that most people never get an opportunity to see the world, so I figured I should maybe think about my options a little more."

"Really?" Tulia said, forgetting to play it cool.

"That's great," I said. "Hey — *you* were the one who said that stuff."

"I know. I was really smart."

I punched him on the arm. "You're an ass." He grinned as they helped me stow the kayak.

⚓

Tulia and Isaac were on shipshape duty, so the rest of us took the dinghy ashore. Jimmy and Christine were making the rounds of the grocery stores, Mat had official duties, but Martin and I were free for the morning. There were a set of walking trails at the other end of town where some of the other cruisers said they saw pink flamingos and lots of iguanas. I was ready for a good walk so we decided to see if we could find them.

We all walked into town, leaving Jimmy and Christine at the first shop. "What do you have to do?" Martin asked Mat.

She sighed. "There's an obscene amount of paperwork you have to do just to leave. I already spent a whole day checking in and now I get to do it all over again to check out." She rolled her eyes. "The burden of command."

We dropped her off at the *Capitanía*, a small hut near the commercial dock that already had an ominous-looking queue of people waiting and brandishing sheaves of paper. "If I'm still here when you're on your way back, bring me a sandwich."

We agreed and walked along the waterfront according to the directions we'd gotten. The street was lined with bars, restaurants and small hostels and there were cheesy "Iguana Crossing" signs up at the intersections. It was already steamy hot and it would only get worse as the sun rose higher. I pulled a large bottle of water from my bag, took a slug and passed it over to Martin. He still hadn't made a decision about staying aboard, but at least we were talking again.

We found the trail head and walked along the neat path lined with spindly trees. It wasn't long before we came to a clearing that held a pond and the famous pink flamingos. "They don't look real," Martin said. "I sometimes wonder if this all just a crazy hallucination."

"Naw," I said, bending down to use the hem of my tank top to wipe the sweat off my face. "It's too hot to be a dream." I took some photos with my phone and watched as a giant iguana scampered along the path we'd just walked up. "Though I take your point." We followed the lizard's route back to the main road and stopped at one of the bars for a cold drink.

It must have been a couple of hours since we'd left Mat at the Port Captain's, but she was still there when we passed by. "Are you okay?" Martin asked.

She'd put on a ridiculous floppy hat and still looked like she was melting. "The internet is down so they can't issue our *Zarpe*, but I don't want to leave because it's still first come first served and if I lose my place I'll have to start all over again."

I pulled my phone out and confirmed that the island's wifi was, indeed, not connecting. "Can we use our satellite connection on the Bucket to get whatever they need?"

Mat shook her head. "It's the government system. This happens all the time and usually it's back up in a few minutes. I'll just wait. But can you get me something to eat? And a *refresco* or something cold?" She handed us a wad of bills.

"Sure." We went across the street to the restaurant. They'd chosen their location cleverly, as it was filled with mariners waiting their turn at the office across the way. We brought a sack of takeout back to Mat and offered to keep her company.

"No, I still intend to leave tomorrow and there's plenty to be done aboard before we go. I'll manage on my own, now that I won't die of starvation." She bit into the sandwich to punctuate her point, so we made our way back to the dinghy dock.

It was well after noon when we got back and Martin went to go do something — either help out with the boat chores or pack up his gear to leave; I didn't ask. I went down to the servers and checked on them. They weren't very happy with the crummy wifi, so I set them manually to use only our satellite. We'd be relying on it full-time anyway soon enough. The thought gave me pause. I'd only been on the boat for two weeks and now we'd be spending probably longer than that on a single passage. It was scary, but the crew was good. I'd learned to trust Mat and Isaac, and the rest knew their stuff. It would be fine. It would be an adventure. There was no reason to panic.

If I kept telling myself that, maybe I'd eventually believe it.

⚓

Martin was still aboard at dinner, which made me share a significant glance with Tulia over our steaks and salad. Neither of us said anything. Superstition, again. All of us were more subdued than usual, a feeling of expectation in the air. The boat was as tidy as I'd ever seen it and when Isaac deflated the dinghy and secured the outboard all of a sudden it felt real. We were leaving in the morning, really heading off to sea.

"I guess that's that," Martin said as I watched Isaac stow the deflated dinghy down below. "I'm not going anywhere now."

"You could take a kayak," I said. "Get someone to come with you and tow it back."

"Naw, that wouldn't work," he said, though we both knew it would. "I guess I'm stuck here." He shrugged. "Oh, well."

I looked toward the shore, the penguins quietly waddling about the rocks, iguanas dozing in the fading sun, boobies and other seabirds circling overhead.

"Oh, well," I echoed. "Who needs land, anyway?"

I am deeply grateful to the following people who helped with this book and the entire series:

★ Erica L. Satifka, my editor, for her careful and wise comments;
★ Amanda Witherell, for convincing me that writing about sailing was cool;
★ Dawn Bonanno, S.B. Divya, Elizabeth Shack, and others, for their thoughts on an early draft;
★ the Codex writers' group, for too much to mention;
★ all the sailors and local people I met on my travels, for sharing their lives and stories;
★ and my mate, Steven Ensslen, for everything.

Darusha Wehm is the author of the *Devi Jones' Locker* series and is the editor of the crime and mystery journal *Plan B Magazine*. She is also a published poet.

Writing as M. Darusha Wehm, she is the author of five published science fiction novels, including the award-nominated *Andersson Dexter* cyberpunk mystery series. Her short science fiction has been published in many venues, including *Escape Pod*, *Mothership Zeta* and several anthologies.

She lives in Wellington, New Zealand after sailing down the west coast of the Americas and across the Pacific Ocean with her partner, Steven, on their sailboat, Scream.